Winifred Jennings Cowley

Lorin Mooruck

And other Indian stories

Winifred Jennings Cowley

Lorin Mooruck
And other Indian stories

ISBN/EAN: 9783337304010

Printed in Europe, USA, Canada, Australia, Japan

Cover: Foto ©Andreas Hilbeck / pixelio.de

More available books at **www.hansebooks.com**

LORIN MOORUCK;

AND OTHER INDIAN STORIES.

BY

GEORGE TRUMAN KERCHEVAL.

BOSTON:

J. STILMAN SMITH & CO.,

3 HAMILTON PLACE.

1888.

INTRODUCTORY LETTER.

—◦◇◦—

IT will interest the readers who are far from the frontier to know the impression made by these stories upon those whose lives have thrown them into close relations with the American Indians.

The following letter is from Bishop Whipple of Minnesota, whose life has been so largely given to the elevation of the Indian tribes.

It would certainly add to the interest of the book if readers know that the stories are not merely founded on fact in a general way, but that the incidents described are substantially true. For obvious reasons the real names of parties referred to are not printed, but the reader may be assured that there has been no exaggeration for the artistic purpose of heightening the effect.

E. E. HALE.

PREFACE.

I HAVE been asked to write a preface to this book. As I read these sad stories, it recalled the weary days of my first visits to the Indian country, where I saw pictures of degradation and sorrow, and heard stories of oppression and wrong which would appall the stoutest heart. No Christian could look on such scenes, and not cry out as David Livingstone did in Africa, "O God! when will this great sore be healed?"

The North American Indian is the noblest type of a wild man on the earth. He believes in a Great Spirit, he has an unquestioned faith in a future life, he has a passionate love for his children, and will lay down his life for his people.

The government of the United States inherited from colonial days a mischievous Indian policy. The scattered colonists could not ask Red Men, who outnumbered them a hundred to one, to become their wards. Therefore they recognized these nomadic tribes as Indian nations, sovereign people living within our borders, not subject to our laws, with no personal rights of property, no homes, and no government.

We knew their chiefs had only advisory power, and were simple leaders of a savage clan ; when civilization had destroyed their game, we builded almshouses to train up savage paupers, we allowed evil influences to drag them down to a depth of degradation their heathen fathers had never known. The agent was appointed as a reward for political service, and he accepted his office to acquire a fortune on a salary of fifteen hundred dollars a year. The white settlers coveted the Indian's land, and every treaty had behind it those who desired to use the Indian as a key to unlock the public treasury. There is always on the frontier a class of reckless men who wantonly commit acts of violence against Indians.

The Indian knows no law but the "lex talionis"— "an eye for an eye," "life for life." The blow falls on the innocent, and the guilty escape. A Christian Indian woman died by the violence of white men — a brutal mixed-blood killed an Indian woman in the presence of three others. The Indians arrested him, and took him to the nearest fort. He was put in the guard-house ; after three months the Secretary of War ordered his discharge, because there was no law to punish an Indian murderer. If an Indian is suspected of committing crimes of violence against whites, lynch law usually settles the matter without judge or jury.

Behind every Indian war there are causes which

would arouse the indignation of any civilized nation. I mention only one. An officer of the United States Army was crossing a desert country with border men as guides. They came to an Indian village. There was no one in the village but children. The kind-hearted officer gave the children food, and filled their calabashes with water. Later in the day he missed his guides; and when they came into camp at evening he asked, "Where have you been?" "To fix those Indian papooses." "What did you do?" "We threw them over the precipice and killed them: nits make lice."

Thank God, the heart of the nation has been touched. There is hope of entire reform. We cannot bring back the dead or undo the record which is a stain upon our nation: we can do justly. Congress has passed the Dawes severalty bill, which provides for personal rights of property and future citizenship. The law will not execute itself. Citizenship is a blessing only to men prepared for it. In the old territorial days there was a law which gave Indians the right to vote who wore civilized dress. I have heard of a cunning mixed-blood who passed a whole tribe of Indians through one hickory shirt and trousers between sunrise and sunset. The Indian must have the protection of law, but not law administered as it was by white men to the men of Wallowa.

The Indian Bureau is a thousand-fold better than

no guardianship. This reform needs and must have the best efforts, the wisest care of the largest-hearted men of the nation, or "the last state will be worse than the first."

I believe under such a commission as that recommended by President Cleveland this blessed work will be accomplished.

If these stories of George Truman Kercheval shall deepen the sympathy and love which goes before all effort for the helpless, the author will be overpaid.

H. B. WHIPPLE,
Bishop of Minnesota.

FARIBAULT, MINNESOTA,
February, 1888.

CONTENTS.

LORIN MOORUCK.

CHAPTER I.

THE VILLAGE OF NATSEE.

THE mountains rose in wild confusion as
if suddenly awakening from the warm em-
brace of volcanic fires, turned their dull, silent
peaks to the wide heavens, and lived in perpetual torpor, while at their feet danced the mad
river, foaming and frothing in its eager haste to
pass between these grim monitors out to the
blue ocean, but crag and boulder, bottomless
gulch and sharp horn of mountain, tumbled it
hither and yon as it rushed to the sea. Lorin
Mooruck, lying at full length upon a jutting
rock above, wondered if civilization were not
like this wild child of the mountain, whose birth
was up somewhere near the clouds, whose life
was passed in fretful impatience at obstruction,
whose end was to lose itself in the broad ocean
and be part of the perpetual blue pendulum
swung ever to and from the eternal sands, each

wave wearing a crested cap like every other
wave.

A close observer would have found something
in each cap differing from another, but Lorin
viewed them from afar and thought, "Here in
the village one lives a different life."

The sun has not yet set as the youth dreams
on. Back of him lies the village: houses tossed
here and there along the mountain side, some
with latticed porch or high gabled roof; houses
with open fire-places where burns the resinous
pine; houses with curtained windows where the
sun ever seeks and finds admittance; for here
are no deep-tinted carpets to fade with light,
but white pine floors and uncushioned, straight-
backed chairs. Little gardens of beans, pota-
toes, and corn are fenced in near many of the
homes. In Natsee the women divide the labor
with the men. They dress and dry the salmon
caught in the innumerable eddies and back cur-
rents of the restless stream, they gather acorns
for meal, and come from the pine depths with
arms full of sprigs and branches to sputter on
the broad hearth. The old men cultivate patches
of ground or mend the fishing nets, the young
men work in the lumber mills at Tarcata, or
look after the hogs and horses. Along the
river are the fisheries and stagings to hold the
fishermen and their nets.

Home is very dear to these people, and they form a happy community. On either side of this turbulent stream are dotted villages like Natsee, where tribal law has given place to individual interests, little worlds where love and sorrow, happiness and despair, creep in and point the victim to begin the puppet show; and here one sees a smiling face hiding a heavy heart, a placid face, and behind it a satisfied shiftlessness, all a part of the great whole where the soul stands aloft and the body moves under the mask.

Mooruck dreams until the mountain heights blush with the kiss of the royal light as it curves in brilliancy and dies in radiance, leaving its soft remembrance upon their snowy peaks, until the clouds above grow gray and chill. The crescent shroud, whose lord has disappeared, begins to glow with expectancy of reaching him, and as she moves aloft the stars are lit to guide her on, and Mooruck wonders if the heavens have no pity for her sorrow, when suddenly some one calls in his ear, " You are lazy, Lorin !"

It is only Meetah, a girl a few years younger than he, in a short gown, her black hair loosened to her waist. The dream-light fades from his eyes, he rises and shakes himself somewhat like a Newfoundland dripping from the cool river, and turns to Meetah, who has curled herself near on the rock.

"I suppose you were making dream-tales, as usual," she said contemptuously. "What a pity you could not ride on the tail of the moon and find out why the stars are all a-glitter. You might be willing to work then and stop your dreaming."

"I cannot help it, Meetah," he said slowly; "the mountains call me, and when the sun dies I must see that scarlet touch he leaves behind. Did you never notice the singing in the river that dashes there — hear the music — I can never give up trying to catch it;" and he dropped on the rock near her, leaning over to listen.

"Lorin Mooruck, you will never amount to that!" — she snapped her fingers at him.

He smiled; he was used to her impatience.

She meant he should care that she thought him stupid, so she announced, "Elmer Stone has gone to Tarcata to work in the mill; he will have twice as much money as you, before the moon comes again."

Her words seemed to have no effect, for Mooruck answered, "What do I care for the money — my mother is old — the garden keeps us — the pipes that I carve get us enough to wear, and when that is not enough, I mend the fish nets — what more does one want?"

"And that is all you care?" she asked, her black eyes flashing.

"When it is needed, I will do more." His dim gaze wavered over the mountains that worked their deathless charm upon him.

For a moment, Meetah was silent. Her eyes rested upon his supple, strong, young form, his deep-browed eyes, his sharply defined features, his short, dark hair pushed back from his wide forehead, but instantly her impatience returned as his thoughts wandered. "You are dreaming away the present, you are drifting out into the future, Lorin; nothing is sure to you, 'tis for me." She arose; the rugged mountains outlined her girlish form, as, folding her arms, she said impressively, "I am going away to the world."

Mooruck turned quickly and looked at her.

"My mother is dead, my father sleeps also — you have all been kind to me, here in the village. Soon, my sister, Hannah Tocare, will be Hannah Moore. Then — Joseph Moore will be enough for her. There is no one to need me here. I am going out into the East. Some day I shall come back; then —"

"What do you mean!" exclaimed Mooruck, suddenly springing up, alive with energy.

Meetah thought joyously, "Some beautiful spirit must have looked like that!"

Mooruck's dream-tales had awakened her artistic nature, but she never quite admitted it, even to herself.

These friends had grown up from childhood together; she, eager, impatient, full of animal spirit; he, quiet, reticent, usually by himself, moulding odd figures out of the red clay; but the sound of Meetah's childish laughter always brought a smile to his lips. He heard it amidst all the sound and noisy play of other children; her life seemed strung in tune with his. As they grew older they understood each other without explanations. Meetah was fifteen now, Lorin almost two years older.

As Meetah grew, her mind turned to practical affairs, though her best enjoyment was to sit by the side of her young playmate on the cliff in the stillness of twilight, and listen to his wonderful tales of the heavens, the mountain gods, the people who lived under the sea, and the white-faced maidens in the river that dashed at their feet. The villagers were proud of Mooruck's skill in carving; his kind, old, wrinkled-faced mother would smile, and say their house had been built by Mooruck's pipes. Eight years ago the garrison people had lived near, and they took as many of his curiously carved red clay pipes, with long, slender handles, as he could carve in days and weeks; but the Fort had been moved; there was no need of a garrison near Indians who quietly supported themselves and had always been friendly. In place of the garrison came settlers, who thought there was little room in this country for any one not a foreign immigrant. They saw no need for Indians to live in a village like this, the land was too good; and so they tried to make trouble by encroaching upon the village. They had no use for carved pipes, so Mooruck made very little with his carving now. He mended fish nets, and did it so dexterously that his friends would have supplied him always with that, but that he had a passion for the carving. Sometimes it seemed to Meetah that the little figures had been there all the time, that Lorin heard their cry and let them come out, as he cut away obstructive clay. No one knew that she had a little sandy horse, with four stumps and no tail, ridden by a legless boy, put carefully among her few treasures. Lorin made it when only four years old.

Meetah's impatience was caused by her love for him, her heroic ideas of what he might do. She wanted all people to know he was a hero, though they thought him a dreamer. In her father's day she heard strange tales of adventure and bravery, and she longed to be a son, that she might ride forth and accomplish some daring deed that would make people wonder.

When about twelve years old she deliberately burned her arm with a heated iron to find out her power of endurance, and all through the painful healing she never complained.

Another friend of Meetah's was Elmer Stone, a keen-eyed, broad-shouldered youth, with a determination to succeed in being as well off as any rich ranchman; he had gone recently to work in the lumber mills at Tarcata. When Mr. Tuscan, the kind-hearted minister, had spoken of the villagers to Colonel Frost, who came out from Washington, he had pointed to Elmer as showing the Indian civilization had developed. He spoke of him as a representative man, who would one day leave the village and be part of the great world beyond. Meetah stood there, her black eyes shining with defiance. It was not hard then to see whether she cared for Elmer or Lorin best. She determined to go into the great world herself; she would see what it was like. Lorin should go too. Mr. Tuscan had been glad of her wish to go; he said he would try and get her a place at the Q—— school in the East, where she might advance in her work, for already she would take fine stitches in sewing, and knew all that they taught in the village school. All her people spoke English, and it had not been difficult for her to follow the text-books. Any one in the village could talk

and understand English, though they preferred
to use their own language among themselves.   If
the school were a good place for one, it would be
a good place for another.   Oh, if she could only
awake some fire in Lorin, some wild life that
would stir him up to dissatisfaction.   She had
been thinking of going a long time now, and to-
day Mr. Tuscan had received word from Q——.
He had told her not an hour since, and her first
thought had been to find Lorin.   She was filled
with the excitement of anticipation, but here
was Lorin, dreaming away the time as though
nothing was to happen.

   When he sprang up, Meetah clasped her
hands and cried : "Ah! Lorin, you will come at
last!"   Then she went on rapidly : "I am going away to the school at Q——.   They will
teach us both — you will come too — they will
teach us everything.   We will go out into the
great world — you shall be the representative
man.   You will not stay here in the village,"
pointing to where she turned her eyes at the
shadowy outline of their homes; "but," she
added softly, "not forever, never forever, Lorin
— we will remember how they loved us — we
will come back — all we do shall be for them."
Then quickly, "Mr. Tuscan says he can get a
place for you — let me tell him to write?"

   Slowly he raised his eyes to hers, then turned

away toward a glimmer of light in the village. "That is my mother's home — my father's grave is here. I cannot leave these for a small spot crowded with white men. The heavens arch over us here — they tell me that the white man cannot see the heavens from his home — he journeys away every year to breathe fresh air and see the sky — I think the Great Spirit guards us better here."

"For the sake of an arching sky you will lose everything? The white man will take your home and laugh at your right; they will drive you from the village — in that day you will dig in the ground for roots to keep you from starving — it is coming — they will creep upon you before you know it. I have not been to school and heard the teachers talk for nothing. Lorin, will you stay and be treated worse than a wild goat? I have more spirit than that!" She hurled her contemptuous words off in a breath.

"I shall guard my father's grave and fight for my people," he answered gravely.

"Yes," she burst forth, "but what good will it do? the village will be taken by white men and you will be killed likely. I shall go East and learn a better way. I love my people as much as you do, Lorin; the time to fight has passed, we must learn faster the civilized way — white people think we are ignorant of their way.

I shall get all the knowledge that I can, then I shall come back and teach others."

"You have a fine dream, Meetah," he smiled. "You want to be like the man and woman whose word is not to be believed."

She came swiftly toward him and putting her hand upon his arm raised her eyes to his, saying eagerly, "Lorin, *when* did I ever lie to you?"

He moved away, her hand fell from his sleeve.

"Not yet, but the sun falls over the mountains there, sometimes early, sometimes late, but they are used to it and do not know the difference. You will find it easy to learn new ways; you will think one thing to-day and another thing to-morrow; your lips will say it, and like our mountains there you will not know that the shadow has come — you will put yourself in the way of change. It will be a long road between you and the village, then. Go if you like; I remain here."

A doubt seized her, she was filled with questioning fear; she had come to him buoyant with hope — he had painted all away in dismal colors.

"I shall not change in my soul — it will be always the same as yours; can't you feel that, Lorin — "

"Will you forget to eat, and talk here forever?" came a voice up the hill. It was Hannah Tocare, who had come for her sister, and now would not wait to let them talk.

"Good-by, Lorin," said Meetah, mournfully, as she turned away.

Somehow his voice did not come and he watched them in silence as they wound down the mountain side and disappeared in the distance; then he threw himself at full length along the rock, dug his fingers in the brown lichen and wondered if Meetah would, in truth, leave the village.

CHAPTER II.

THE MASTER WORKMAN.

THE tourist will tell you that the town of Crespy sprang up in the night-time. They call it a mushroom growth, and truly, for the velvety, pale-colored mushroom has a lining of dark tint deeply ridged; so also has Crespy, its history being deeply lined with dark facts. The town was stolen bit by bit, under cover of right, but by dint of wrong, and the workmen will sometimes laughingly point at the tall, olive-hued stone-cutter in their midst and call him Mooruck of Crespy, for his father was once chief of a people who owned this land. It was, not long since, part of the ground belonging to the people of Natsee, and is still theirs by law, but no one cares to enforce their rights, no one cares for the Indian's title here.

As the workmen gather in the low-roofed saloon at night, they laugh at the idea of Mooruck, the Indian, owning land, and among themselves they say : —

" He is a good fellow, after all, a master workman — but the Lord knows where he learned it all!"

A newly arrived Pole muttered, "From the devil, perhaps," but a powerful Swede arose with: "None of that!   We know Lorin Mooruck and none shall say a word against him while I'm here, no matter what he is."

"Bully for you, Bill," burst forth one of the crowd.   "He's a good 'un if 'e is a Injun — we'll say that much."

"I ain't over much fond of 'em," said a thin man as he sipped the contents from a broken mug, "but I've a good word for 'im, for when I shied wurk las' spring, 'cause the ol' 'oman wus sick, 'e did m' wurk un 'is too, wurkin' after 'ours, an' never a cent did 'e keep, but let th' boss turn over m' pile same as usual."

"He don't keer for this crowd much," ventured a good-natured frontiersman.

"Wal," said one, "he's got the good sense ter know that poor whiskey makes an Injun crazy, an' it ain't much good yer can find in these yere parts."

"But the devil's own knows where he goes nights," muttered an Irishman.

"Leave the devil to find out then," growled the broad-shouldered Bill; and no one caring to dispute with him, the conversation changed.

There were a few good houses in Crespy and many more building.

One day, Miss Slater, daughter of the builder, took a party of friends down to see the stone-cutters at work, but from the whispered words, no one knew they had come down to see but one of these men; at her request, Mr. Harrold, the artist, who had a couple of rooms in the Slater's house, accompanied them, and while they talked he took a hasty sketch of the tall stone-cutter with the short, dark hair and olive skin. His costume pleased the artist: the light brown overalls, the pale blue shirt, the red handkerchief knotted about the throat, the head without covering, the broad shoulders, the strong, steady stroke of the hammer, — the picturesque whole delighted Mr. Harrold. The man gave close attention to his work, and seemed unconscious of their presence. The artist came to see the stone-cutters again, and yet again, each time· talking longer with this skilful workman, whose unerring eye, steady aim and muscular strength placed him above his fellows. At first, Mr. Harrold came merely because Miss Slater wished it, but finally he came because he, too, was interested in this young Indian; so it happened that Mooruck never spent his evenings in the low saloon.

Miss Slater or Mr. Harrold might have an-

swered the curiosity of the workmen, but who
would think of asking them?

There was one circumstance that would forever prevent Mooruck's co-laborers from bear-
ing him a grudge. Although he was the master workman, he could never keep good wages
out of their hands, for his employer gave him
less than the unskilled German ; in a way it was
doing the workman harm, though they little
dreamed it, but the very indignation that burned
through Mooruck's veins at such treatment
made him resolve that one day his employer
should stand beneath him, one day he should
see that the law would protect the Indian.

Mr. Pinkham was a grasping Westerner, a
mean man by nature. Part of his creed was to
cheat whom he could ; Mooruck must have the
work, and so for the time being Mr. Pinkham
took the profits.

The fire for which Meetah had longed was
at last kindling Lorin's ambition, but in these
days she worked patiently and sadly, hearing
very little of Lorin. Often, as she sat sewing
in Hannah Tocare's house in the village, she
would try and picture to herself what he did,
what he thought; groping through space, her
heart aglow with love, she felt her thought must
reach him, must awake in return some thought
of her, must put aside distance ; there must be

some power by which her soul could reach his.
Surely he was thinking of her, all barrier of distance had fallen away, her soul should feel his
— was reaching his —

Alas for the passionate women who sit and
dream !

Meetah had been out in the world ; she had
even gone to Massachusetts and worked in a
farmer's family there. She had been the one
girl studying in a class with eleven boys, all
having finished their course of three years, but
so eager for another year of hard work that
after much urging the authorities at Q—— had
granted their desire. At the end of the four
years she read an essay comparing the women
of her race to-day with those of the past. It
had been published in the commissioner's Indian report and sent to the Secretary of the
Interior to impress the nation with the advance-
ment of at least one Indian. But all through
her triumphant last days at school, the praise of
the teachers, the admiration of the visitors, had
fallen upon dull ears ; for in her pocket she carried a badly written letter from the village, telling that Lorin's mother was dead, his house had
been seized by a settler, and he had gone away
to work in a new town. Her sister's husband
had been told he did not own their home ; he
had been driven forth, and a fence put about his

vegetable garden.   He had been warned that, if
he took so much as a bean, he would be com-
mitted to trial for theft from an honest white
man, who intended to use his house, and who
saw fit to take his small farm.   A month had
gone by, two months, and their home was shut
in darkness; no one occupied it.

Meetah had changed in mind; she had im-
proved in character, but her heart was the same.
She smiled in bitterness at her ambition; what
had it brought?   How often she had laughed at
Lorin for dreaming, yet his dream-world might
come nearer true than hers.

Two upper rooms in the Slater's house served
for Mr. Harrold's home.   In the front were
comfortable easy-chairs, pictures without frames,
finely sculptured arms, feet, and heads hanging
against the wall, a high tier of shelves filled
with books, bits of statuary here and there,
draped curiously with fish nets, bits of silk and
pieces of richly colored crêpe.   Out of this
room opened the L-shaped apartment he pleased
to term his workshop.

In the front room, one frosty night, before
the log fire upon the hearth, sat Mr. Harrold
and the master stone-cutter, whose picturesque
dress had given place to a conventional brown
suit ; the two men were good friends, and

Mooruck had been calling up his past life at Mr. Harrold's desire.

The old dreaminess again possessed him as he said slowly, "The strong influence of another life has filled the gap in mine."

If Meetah's eager longing had been gratified, she might have felt his soul then, and trembled.

"There is another force beside my own. Of my own will, even after my mother's death, I would not have left the village. I drank in this force as flowers the sunshine, as leaves the dew. I never knew I took it until one day —" He paused ; his eyes seemed to filter the light from the fire as, turning to Harrold with a startled motion, waving his hand — "It was gone ! Like a bird it opened its wings and fled — it sought the heights, while I lay dreaming. All my life it had been near and I had not known."

He turned and silently watched the ashes as they fell from the burning logs.

There was not sufficient sympathy between Mr. Harrold and Lorin for the former to under- stand what he meant, but using tact the artist asked : —

"So it was not of your own accord that you left the village ?"

"My friend had gone away," answered Lorin, "to find a better way of life, so I, too, decided to go forth and learn the better way also. I

did not wish to go far — I came here — I have
worked, but have learned no better way to live
than that taught by our good Mr. Tuscan —
after all, our simple village life seems best to
me.   Mr. Pinkham has found me of use, but
you, my friend, you have been all the village, all
the mountains, the sky, the singing birds to
me!" He sprang up enthusiastically and placed
his hands on Mr. Harrold's shoulders. "You
have given me a new life. In all my thought
was never such kindness as this. I meant only
to be a good stone-cutter, but you — you have
taught me a different and better work."

"I do not deserve your thanks," said Mr.
Harrold. "If I have taught you the use of
tools, you have taught me how to hold ideas.
But come, I presume you are already impatient
— a change of suit, then to work!"

Stepping upon a chair and reaching up to a
square closet door in the wall, Mr. Harrold
flung from it a couple of shabby overalls and
two worn blue shirts. Donning these costumes,
the jean shirts over the trousers in Chinese
fashion, the men were in working suit. Mr.
Harrold adjusted a light cloth cap to his scant
blonde hair and they then passed on into the
L-shaped room.

It was well lighted by bracket-lamps, and on
one side of the carpetless room, against the
wall, rested a rough, grayish piece of marble,

and near it a trough of wet clay. Scattered on a table near were numerous wooden hammers and fine tools used in marble cutting; a statue half issued from a marble block at the end of the room.

Mooruck hastened to a dark object on a table in the centre of the room and carefully unwrapped from wet cloths the head and bust of a woman in clay. Holding the damp covering in one hand he stepped back and gazed at his work. The deep-set eyes were full of fiery purpose, the long, straight hair was pushed back from a broad, low brow, the lips parted as if for noble utterance, — but it was the expression in the raised eyes that held one speechless.

Harrold stood, for an instant, back of Mooruck, in silence. " I always feel like uncovering before those eyes," he said; and even as he spoke he held his cap in his hand. " You have imprisoned a soul there."

But Mooruck did not hear, he was lost in thought. Presently the Indian started at the sound of hammer on steel and click of marble, for Harrold had passed on and was at work upon the issuing figure at the end of the room. The sound of the tool was like the burst of martial music to the ears of a warrior. Instantly, Lorin flung aside the bunch of wet rags in his hand and in a moment more was at work upon the half-formed shoulders of his statue,

CHAPTER III.

UPON THE MOUNTAIN.

ON one of the hills in the village of Natsee is perched a little cottage of four rooms, the home of Joseph Moore, the fisherman; the household is managed frugally to keep the wolf from the door, for little can Joseph earn, though he fishes all the day and helps Hannah mend the nets at night. She cultivates the little patch of ground at the back of the house, and her sister, Meetah Tocare, helps in the house-work, and of her scanty earnings at the village school gives more than half for the home spending. Hannah and Joseph need all they can have now to keep from starving this coming winter; the ground about their house is newly planted and will not yield well this year. The house and farm from which they were driven last year stand idle; no one uses the house, and the man who claimed the place has taken all the produce, but has not troubled to prepare the land again. Joseph and Hannah have begun their new home with lack of hope, for they do not know how soon they may be driven away from this too,

The white men send their herd quite into the village to graze; there are many Indian farms lost, many homes ruined, many cattle branded with the white man's mark, many a house taken possession of, as a lawless white shows forged papers giving him the right to the home. Yet no one who has authority interferes; people go there with the desire and resolve to cheat these Indians, and when they have robbed them they think they have done a cunning thing. "The Indian will not understand that he has been wronged, he does not know enough," they reason; meanwhile the Indian plans and wonders how to live peaceably and avert all this misery.

As the day wears on, Meetah comes home from the school and sits now in the living-room, her foot rocking the cradle of the sleeping child, while her busy needle flies in and out, as she tries to find some way of escape from their many difficulties.

The child of boisterous animal spirit is lost in this quiet, sad-faced woman, who, though kind and gentle, seems always in deep thought. The children love her and cling about her skirts as they come from the village school, she walking bare-headed in their midst, her large hat swinging on her arm. Of old the people knew when Meetah passed, by the quick step and ringing laugh, but now it is the chattering and merri-

ment of village children, who tell her coming,
and one old woman within doors will tell another
as she listens, "Meetah must be going by from
school."

At her door-step she waves them good by,
and as they scurry down the hill they turn back
with smile and nod to see if she still is there.

To-night as the twilight falls she pushes her
work aside in weary impatience and goes out
into the low-roofed kitchen to help Hannah.
But the work is done; Hannah is waiting supper for Joseph, who will not be home until late,
so Meetah, telling her she will go for a short
walk, throws the little red shawl about her
shoulders and goes out into the twilight towards
the cliff where she and Mooruck dreamed away
the hours in their childhood days, before they
had grown high enough to touch the sorrows
that their parents bore.

The mountains lift their gray heads toward
the changing clouds as of old, and the silvered
tips of the highest peaks gleam in the fading
light. The stream rushes on in its turbulent
course, and the jutting crags hang over, vainly
trying to catch their image in the waters beneath. As Meetah's accustomed feet climb the
mountain side, her thoughts pluck back the
filmy veil about her childhood days : her father
comes forth, strong and brave, the first man in

the tribe to unite with the church, and content only when his children were being educated — but then comes the day when the mission school was closed and a ward politician came out to be their agent. She did not know the meaning of ward politician then; she shivered at the mention of it, and at night covered her head close with the bed-clothes lest she might open her eyes and see him in the room. She smiled now at her childish fancies.

She had always been eager for knowledge; her teacher had taught her to write and rewrite "Knowledge is power," and the good woman thought she was telling the child a wise thing; but Meetah had learned that the use of knowledge was power. In her short life she had seen that knowledge was not power.

Again she remembered when another agent had come and the doors of the mission school had been thrown wide again; if some complaining school-boy could have seen the eager, smiling faces of these Indian children, who were permitted to work and study, how ashamed he might feel at his unwillingness to go to school, when there was no government official to say, "thou shalt," or "thou shalt not learn," no man with power to shut out, by a whim, his future usefulness as a citizen.

As a child, Meetah's strong desire had been

for a good education, that she might be compe-
tent to help her people. While away at school
she had studied housework, the chemistry of
cooking, the art of good dress-making, and,
pleasantest work of all, how to teach others.
But she came back to the village without
money; her own friends went often without
enough to eat, and there seemed little hope.
She applied to be made a teacher at one of the
day schools, but they were run by men sent
from Washington, who refused to employ her.
At last one of these fell ill, and Meetah took
his place. He had received forty dollars a
month, but they gave her twenty-three, "though
she taught very well for an Indian," they said;
so in the morning she taught the older people,
and in the afternoon the children, and in the
evening — I was about to say — she taught the
teachers, for they often came to her in per-
plexity and she graciously helped them; but the
people in authority had an interest in these
teachers and paid them twice as much as the
Indian girl.

The rainbow about her life had been her love
for Lorin. Away at school her thought had
been that he would be proud if she studied and
stood first in her class; he would no longer
think she had done wrong to leave the village;
but now he, too, had left; she had been home a

year and Lorin had not once come back from
this new town. Was he more satisfied there
than in the village? He could read and write,
but he never sent her one word, and she shel-
tered a joyous fancy in her heart that Lorin was
carving out a great future, and when the lines
were well marked he would come and tell her,
for in the past had they not always shared the
same thoughts — and what should hinder in the
future?

Slowly it dawned upon her mind, "Some
other person, some other woman should hinder
in the future." She caught her breath, she
tried to smother the thought, she made an effort
to recall the past — his looks, his smiles, his
words — but this new thought blurred them
from sight, and for the first time she pitied
Elmer Stone.

She had felt sorry for him when she told him
she could not return his love; that she felt how
good and noble he was, but that she could
think no more of him than she did now — but
she had not realized then his feeling; she had
only thought, "How impossible that I could
marry Elmer!" Now — a tear rolled down her
cheek as she remembered his deep sigh — a
selfish tear, for she was grieving at her own
sorrow. Perhaps Lorin would never come — the
time seemed very long — but there was work

for her to do — plenty of work. Live for others — yes, that is what she must do.

If she could find any one to publish what she wrote, she could tell the world about this little village of honest men and women shut in among the mountains, while white men surrounded them like sharks, taking their homes one by one, in all ways trying to discourage them and corrupt the women of the village.

"Oh! if I were but stronger in mind and body," she sighed, as she stood looking off at the mountains that Lorin loved. They were merely immovable points of rock rising one above another, — desolate, unchangeable ; how could Lorin love anything so cold and cruel ? He might die of despair at their feet and in silence they would gaze heavenward.

"God alone cares !" she exclaimed, and in her impetuous manner she dropped upon her knees and, with clasped hands and eyes raised, cried, "Father in heaven, give me patience."

A deep "Amen" came from the edge of the rock. Meetah started up in terror, as a man came swiftly toward her with outstretched hands and smiling eyes.

"I thought to find you here by our beautiful mountains !" He spoke triumphantly.

But Meetah trembled, as she said reproachfully, "To think you were so near and yet I did not feel it!" She ended with a deep sob.

"Is it for joy or sorrow, Meetah?" he asked.

"For both, I think — but most for joy," and as they gazed into each other's eyes, they knew a beautiful world lay before them.

Upon the mountain top that night, the important work of their life was forgotten, the words they had thought to speak faded away; the past, the future, was nothing — all happiness centred in the present, in the simple fact that, at last, they were together.

Impulsively their lips spoke what their hearts had long known; to Meetah, now, the starry dome above was beautiful, the mountains smiled through the misty night veil, and from the waters beneath shone the little stars as though they had come from the deep to greet the stars above.

Lorin felt that his heart would burst for very joy; Meetah had spoken her love in the presence of the beautiful mountains that brooded over the village he loved.

Presently he said, as they turned to leave the cliff and stood upon the edge of the rock, "We cannot live in the village, Meetah; I have left it forever. I did not think so at first, I did not believe I could leave it forever. Do you remem-

ber that night we talked here long ago? I, a
foolish boy, and you, a brave-hearted girl — I
did not know then how you were that better
part of me, without which my life would never
come so near the good and true. I was grieved,
angry, fretful that you were going away — my
terrible loss came over me afterward — but now
— " He smiled radiantly at her.

Looking solemnly up at him, she asked, "Are
you sure that you love me better than any one
in the world, Lorin? Ah! you cannot understand what my love for you is — it is my life.
I feel as though I had always known you better
than you knew yourself — you were not conscious of your own power; you are a great artist
now."

"Only a beginner, my dear one. You are a
dream-child, Meetah; you throw a wonderful
thought around everything. You are the best
part of me; your thought creates my ideal. Will
it not be beautiful to work always together?
My love for you has been the best growth of my
life." He drew her to him. "Together we will
not fear to brave the world."

Even at that moment a faint dread came to
Meetah, a quivering doubt that sometimes shad-
ows great happiness. For a moment she was
silent, then, gently taking his face between her

hands, she pressed a kiss upon his beardless lips and, springing away, cried, " Oh, I am so proud of you, Lorin! I think the earth must be Heaven at last, or the clouds have caught us up, or something has taken us above our own lives!"

CHAPTER IV.

HANNAH'S CURIOSITY REMAINS UNSATISFIED.

MUCH surprised were the Moores when Meetah gayly led Lorin in upon them. Joseph
greeted him with affection, but Hannah complained, "Why did you not come to us before
going to the cliff?"

Meetah's eyes smiled into Lorin's, for they
knew why he had chosen their old trysting-place
first.

"Come," said Hannah, "and join us at supper."

But what was meat, or what was drink, to
either of them! Joseph and Hannah might
have fed a hundred such on meal and water,
and they would have arisen satisfied as if from
a royal feast.

Hannah insisted upon making a bed for Lorin
upon the floor of their living-room; but he had
been invited to remain with a friend in the
village, and before nine o'clock he was on his
way to visit Elmer Stone.

After the housework was finished, Meetah
bade Hannah and Joseph good night, and went

to her barely furnished room which opened from the kitchen.

When Hannah had talked to Joseph awhile over Mooruck's past life and future plans, and hushed the child, who had awakened, she suddenly remembered that Lorin had given no satisfactory answer when she asked why he had gone to the cliff before coming to the house of his best friend. Rising with the thought, she opened Meetah's door, and found her sitting on the edge of her narrow bed, lost in dreamy thought. She glanced up in surprise as her sister entered, and drawing her skirts aside made room for her upon the bed, for there were no chairs there. Her blue dress was unloosened, exposing her white cotton chemise and bare chest, — slight covering for so chilly a night; but Meetah earned little, and spent that upon the household and a few books.

"It was strange," said Hannah, seating herself, "that Mooruck went to the cliff before coming here. Do you not believe he thought us good enough friends to come here when entering the village?"

"Yes," said Meetah, slowly pulling the pins from her low knot of black hair. "But it was his favorite place; he loves the mountains and the stream." She spoke caressingly. "It was natural for him to go to them first."

"But where did you meet him?" queried
Hannah.

"I met him there."

"You did not know he was coming?"

"Do you think I would not have told you?"
asked the girl, glancing up in surprise.

"You were gone a long time," complained
the sister. "Was he there when you first came
to the cliff — what kept you so long?"

Meetah stooped to pick up a pin that had
fallen from her long hair. There was the gleam
of glittering steel and a thud upon the bare floor,
as something slipped from her open dress.

"Meetah Tocare! What is that!" exclaimed
Hannah, springing from the bed and standing
back.

"Hush!" said Meetah, picking up the small
hunting-knife and fixing her eyes steadily upon
her sister's face. "It is nothing — I did not
wish you to know. Be quiet, Hannah, and I will
tell you;" for she still continued to utter her
surprise.

"It is nothing at all," Meetah said, holding
the knife in her hand and running her finger
along its sharp edge. "Please be still. Sit
down, and I will tell you," and she pushed the
knife under the edge of her pillow.

Hannah, with wide eyes, seated herself; not
that she was afraid of a hunting-knife, a rifle, or

a revolver, for she could handle any of these dexterously; but she was surprised that Meetah should conceal such a thing in her bosom.

"I am sorry I have to tell you," said Meetah again; "but never fear; no harm will come to me; I am able to care for myself."

"But why do you wear it?" burst forth Hannah.

"It was night before last, as I came through the village, some drunken white men chanced to be near me." Her eyes flashed, and the color sprang into her olive cheeks. "I was an Indian girl; the cowards followed me, uttering insulting words; as I was a woman, and alone, I fled before them; but," nervously grasping the knife and springing up, "if I had had this then, I would have *killed* them!"

She threw it away from her, far over on the bed. "It makes my blood seethe to remember it! Had I been a man I would have throttled the words down their ugly throats. To-day I got that!" She seated herself quietly. "When it is necessary, I can use it."

"What shall we do! what shall we do!" wailed Hannah, thoroughly overcome by the danger.

"Nothing," said Meetah, scornfully. "Do anything, and you will bring on an Indian war." She laughed. "*These red devils are such cut-*

throats—that's what you will hear. We are all
red-handed, bloodthirsty savages — all — there
is no difference!" She paused a moment, add-
ing solemnly, "Let the Father above take account of the white savages."

"What can we do! *What* can we do?"
murmured Hannah, clasping and unclasping her
hands, as she swayed her body to and fro.

"Keep silent; that is best. I am sorry I
had to tell you, Hannah." She put her arm
about her sister's neck. "We can do nothing.
Do not fret. Tell no one; above all, never let
Lorin or Joseph know. When I fail to take
care of myself, the Lord will protect me. Do
not fret, Hannah."

"But the danger!" exclaimed Hannah. "As
if you could kill two or three men — as if you,
alone, would not be caught by them."

"They were too drunk to run, Hannah, and
so they could not catch me."

"And you do not know who they were?
What can we do! what can we do!"

"Nothing. Even if I did know who they
were, there is nothing that we could do. If
I were a white girl, it would be different. What
is it to blast the life of an Indian girl!"

"And you do not know any of them?"

"What good would it do?"

Hannah stopped her moody swaying and

looked searchingly at Meetah. "You do know who they were!"

"What if I do?" said the girl, defiantly; "I shall not tell."

"Very well," said Hannah, rising and speaking severely; "I shall find out."

"Oh, no, no, Hannah!" cried the girl, flinging herself before her. "Please, please do not try to find out. It will only bring misery upon us all; Joseph and Lorin will hear of it. They will be killed!"

"What they deserve," said the older sister, sternly.

"You do not understand," said Meetah, fiercely, catching Hannah by the arm. "It is Lorin and Joseph who will be killed! Oh, if you knew what I know!" with a cry of despair. "You stay close in the house and do not know what goes on close outside the village. Promise me — promise you will be quiet!"

Hannah seemed to waver, but she did not answer.

"You shall not go until you promise," said Meetah, firmly.

Suddenly Hannah burst into tears. Meetah tried to soothe and comfort her, but with long-drawn breaths she wailed: "Sometimes I am wild thinking what is right — I promised our dying father to care for you — would you have me break my word — no, no, I will keep it until the stones melt."

"No, Hannah," said the girl, gently, "I would be the last one to ask you to do wrong. You will not forget your promise to our father, — you will care for me better if you keep silent."

"But I gave my word; I said I would protect you always —"

"Yes, yes," said Meetah, caressingly. "You are very good, Hannah — no harm has come yet — wait awhile before you speak."

"Sometimes I am so troubled I cannot think," said Hannah, beginning to dry her eyes. "It was not long since that I knew what was right to do, without trying so hard to think; but now, even you ask me to break my word with our dead."

"Not break your word, Hannah," Meetah protested gently. "You will keep your promise best if you do as I ask."

"Well," Hannah said reluctantly after much entreaty, "it may not be right."

"But it is right," said Meetah as she kissed her good night. "Do not be sad. Some day a better time will come."

In the middle of the night, as Hannah lay awake, she suddenly remembered that she had not yet been told why Mooruck went to the cliff first.

CHAPTER V.

THE MENACE.

MEETAH, in a delicious, half-awake dreaminess, lived over Lorin's plans for the future. . He had told her of his statue, and she smiled happily as she recalled that night, long ago, when she had urged him to leave the village ; for her words and attitude had been so firmly impressed upon his mind, that with his own hands he had made an image of her in clay, picturing her as she stood that night upon the mountain top. He was carving it out from the marble now. She knew where she would first go when she reached Natsee : it would be to Mr. Harrold's studio, where she would see Lorin's work.

Alas ! when she went to Natsee, the studio was the first place to which she rushed in her wild despair.

The sun scarce cast his rays upon the earth when all in the house of Joseph, the fisherman, were up and at work. There was breakfast to get, beds to make, the house to clean, and Joseph's light lunch to prepare that he might take it with him, for the salmon were getting scarce,

and it required careful adjustment of the nets
in the back eddies of the treacherous stream
and a good knowledge of the changeful current
to go abroad in a frail skiff like Joseph's. Then
there was to be the church picnic fifteen miles
from the village, at the cleared forest, a small
flat piece of ground on the edge of the stream.
Saturday had been selected as the best day, so
that teachers and pupils need lose no time at
school. Joseph could not spare the time to go,
much as he would have enjoyed the meeting
and gossiping of friends. Hannah, with the
child, had been promised a seat in a neighbor's
wagon; Meetah had been expected to go in an
old cart with some of the children, but now that
Lorin had come her plans changed.

Before seven o'clock he came to bid her good
morning, but stood for a time near the open
kitchen door, where the sun streamed in, listen-
ing to her rich voice as it floated out to him in
a joyous carol. Presently she came to the door,
wiping her bright dish-pan out and hanging it
on the nail. Lorin no longer stood still; he
told her she looked fresh as a sweet mountain
flower, in her pink dress, and as he stole a morning kiss, she laughingly drew back, telling him
to beware, lest he took the freshness away.

How the swift-winged birds sang that day,
and the royal sun smiled! all for these gay

young lovers, as they rode happily over the hills to the picnic ground, in a reckless old wide-brimmed buggy, behind a hollow-backed mare who stopped every now and then to brush off a fly and look back at these people, who would have been almost unconscious if she had stopped to nibble at the coarse bunches of grass on the hillside.

Lorin was warmly greeted by old and young; all had heard the night before that he was in the village; the old men and women sat and told stories of his childhood, and wondered if he could feel the same toward them, now that he lived among white men.

Mr. Tuscan stood with his back against a tall pine, and pointed with pride to the old and young members of his congregation, as he talked to Mr. Balch, who had come out from the East to see this village community. He could not refrain from expressing his astonishment at these people, who talked English, desired education, were capable of caring for themselves, had framed excellent laws for the village community, were dressed as any villagers on the Atlantic coast, were thoughtful, agreeable, intelligent, awake to their own interests, and most hospitable to him, a stranger. Soon the Rev. Leonard Williams, a native preacher, joined them. He came from the village six miles below, and

worked for his people on Tolstoi's plan. He
earned no salary, but gave all he had, and received in turn the devotion and care of the
people.

At noon the tables were spread with clean,
white linen and damask cloths, and covered with
good tableware, with glassware and castors,
making things look quite homelike to Mr. Balch.
He noticed among all the men, women, and
children, but one barefooted child, the daughter
of a white settler. They were kind to her, and
Meetah saw that the poor little thing did not go
away hungry.

After lunch Mr. Balch was introduced to
Meetah, and she quietly saw his surprise as
she turned the conversation from one topic to
another of world-wide interest. Watching them
on the edge of the forest, stood a tall, broad-
shouldered, thick-lipped man, known as Bob
McHenry. He scowled as he watched Meetah,
for he saw no reason why she should smile
at one white man, and yet show disdain for
another. He faintly remembered her running
away from him a few nights since, but could
not distinctly recall why he had not followed
her. He had thought she detested all white
men ; but now his anger grew as he saw that she
was making friends with this finely dressed ten-
derfoot. When the picnickers arose from the

table, he skulked back among the trees, but not before Lorin's keen eye had studied his every feature.

On the morrow Meetah and Lorin went to the village church, crowded with Christian Indian worshippers, and knelt side by side at the chancel rail, as they received the holy communion from the hands of the good Mr. Tuscan.

As they came home from church, Joseph and Hannah paused abruptly : they had been in deep converse. Their cheerful greeting did not deceive Meetah, who asked immediately what distressed them, and then the whole story came out.

Soon after Lorin and Meetah had left for church, Bob McHenry came in and presented a bill to Joseph Moore for $57. He claimed that Joseph's cattle last year had wandered over his cornfield, and damaged it to twice that extent. Though the bill would have been preposterously ludicrous to a white man who owned but one cow, yet not so to the Indian : the white man might employ an attorney and sue Bob McHenry, but Joseph had no right to sue a white man, either personally or by aid of an attorney, though he owned but one cow and could bring proof that she had been kept in her small fenced yard all the year. This proof was the word of the Indian's, and therefore would not be believed.

Bob McHenry's cattle had been roaming through the village for over a year, destroying cornfields, grain, and vegetable gardens, and all this time the Indians had been trying to get some lawyer to bring the matter into court. Each family had promised to pay five dollars, whether the lawyer won the case or not; but no man would undertake it, and the Indians were obliged to suffer loss.

As Bob McHenry left the house, he made the proposition that if Joseph would give him Meetah, he would call the account square; otherwise, they had best leave their belongings and fly to the mountains, for the stoniest crag in the land would be pleasanter for them than the village, unless the money or Meetah was handed over.

We who live in comfortable homes, protected by the United States law, can with difficulty bring ourselves to realize the cruelty practised by citizens upon these people from whom we have withheld the protection of our law.

It is impossible to portray the feeling of horror and surprise, not unmixed with terror, that made Meetah shiver, and fired Lorin's blood, when this story was told. "There is but one thing to do. We must leave the village," said Hannah, sadly looking about the barely furnished room. "Leave our home, leave all our friends —"

"Not so," said Joseph. "This is our own home, and we will not give it up."

"But that is what you said before," answered Hannah; "we did leave our home; they drove us out in a single night. Here we have but begun to make another. We will not fly to the mountains. We shall all go to Crespy. We can each work. There, if we make a home, perhaps we will be allowed to keep it — to stay in one place. Joseph, we can all work?" she said appealingly, for every one was silent.

"People are very cruel, Hannah," said Meetah, standing beside her, and gently smoothing her glossy hair. "They do not understand yet, that all we desire is to live quietly and work for our daily bread."

"But they must understand that we are Christian men and women here in Natsee," said Hannah. "There, we would have an honest chance. You know we would," turning to Mooruck, who had remained silent, his lips pressed as if in pain, his eyes as though seeking something in the distance. "You yourself told me that all people from different countries were there —"

"Yes," he answered slowly; "there is a place for all — but not for us."

"But what is the difference? why not?" persisted Hannah, her voice pitched high in excitement.

Meetah caught Lorin's questioning glance, and answered, "Yes, Lorin. Tell her."

"The reason why you cannot go there, Hannah, is that two days ago there was an offer made and published in both weekly papers there, an offer of two dollars and a half for the scalp of any Indian. It ended, '*Old pioneers, tempted by the reward for Indian scalps, are out on a hunt for red-skins. Some killing is looked for.*'"

"O God! Is there no mercy anywhere?" cried Hannah, shuddering, and covering her eyes with her hands; worn hands that had carefully carried and gently cared for the white daughter of a sick settler, that had given food to the hungry, that had toiled in a neighbor's field to save the strength of a fast-failing father, that had often folded in prayer for another's good. She had cared for her Master, who said, "Inasmuch as ye did it unto one of these my brethren, even these *least*, ye did it unto me."

"No. There is no mercy," said Lorin. "We do not ask for pity. We ask for the same chance these men have, who offer a reward for our dead. But," as if putting something aside as he raised his hand, "Our Father has given us the chance to be Christian; I hope we will remember that —"

Joseph interrupted him. "The only way is

for us to fight. Because we have always taken
care of ourselves and been peaceable, they think
our spirit is dead ; they have no fear of us ; they
think there is nothing left us but to die : even
rabbits are safer than we. But I shall not leave
the home. I have no money to pay Bob Mc-
Henry. My living is to fish : no white man shall
ever drive me from here."

" It is very hard to understand," said Meetah,
"that the people who were good to me East,
and the people here, who would take from us
all we have, are of the same race."

" It is because we have no right in the law,"
said Mooruck. " If they will but give us the
right, give the right to our people in the village,
we would soon use it. Men pity us, fear us,
hate us ; when we have the law, they will respect us. I do not fear to go back to Crespy
but it would not be safe for you and Joseph to
come yet." Then, in an altered voice, and coming close to Hannah, he said, " I went to the
cliff before I came here last night — I went to
find my bride. Meetah and I can go back together. No harm can happen to us ; I have
good friends there. But it will be best for you
and Joseph not to come just now. Meetah will
be my wife, and you need not mind the threat
of any one."

" No, no ! I would not let her go," moaned

Hannah. "We must pay Bob McHenry the money."

"I am not afraid to go anywhere with Lorin; and, Hannah, you cannot get the money. It would be very sweet to go back with you, Lorin," she said, coming to where he stood and laying her hand fondly upon his arm; "but perhaps we can arrange matters here. Let us go to Mr. Tuscan; he will surely have some way to help us."

They were each glad of her idea, and all went at once to the good man's home. He advised them to wait. Bob McHenry would not make them leave the village just yet, he thought, and in order that he might not put into execution his terrible threat against Meetah, she must come and live with them awhile. He and Mrs. Tuscan both insisted upon this: she could sleep in the room with the children. Meetah said she was not at all afraid, but to please Mooruck she consented to this plan.

Joseph and Hannah went to see some friends in the village, Lorin to make arrangements for leaving early in the morning; and Meetah, taking the child, went home to put her few belongings in a small box; for it had been settled that she should go to Mrs. Tuscan's at sundown.

While the child was made happy with a bright bit of worsted, Meetah put a few underclothes, two or three cotton gowns, and some worn books into the little box; but before she had quite finished, the child became tired and fretful, and, taking it in her arms, she sang a sweet lullaby. After laying the sleeping child in the cradle she started to finish her packing, when the outer door was roughly opened, and Bob McHenry stepped into the room.

Meetah started back, but asked in a low, steady tone, "What is your business?"

"Is that the way you treat your callers!" he exclaimed. "Not over cordial—but never mind, Dumfrey, come on," as he turned to the door he had left open.

In it appeared a tall, thin man with long hair, buckskin trousers fringed at the side, a cartridge belt about his waist, and at his side a pistol and dirk.

CHAPTER VI.

MEETAH LEAVES HOME.

MEETAH saw at a glance that both men were armed, but she stood dauntless, with steady gaze.

"Alone, hey?" queried Bob, with a half leer, as he looked about the room.

"No," said Meetah, "not alone." The blood surged to her brow. Heaven was not far off; she felt strong. The men supposed her wholly at their mercy, but she knew a greater Power guarded her. The helpless child in the crib needed protection also, and this thought gave her courage.

"Don't see nuthin' but the kid," said Dumfrey, laughing, as he pointed to the child asleep.

"If you have come to see Joseph Moore, he is not here," said Meetah, in a harsh voice. "What is your business? speak quickly and go."

"Did you see my bill?" said Bob, with an ugly leer.

Meetah looked steadily at him, but made no reply.

"I saw yer talkin' ter that tender-foot yester-

day, an' thought yer might as well have me as
him. Didn't know as yer'd decided on a white
man before. He's one o' them soft fellers that
couldn't hit a crow." He was slowly drawing
his pistol out, and Meetah quietly watched him.
"But I," he said with gusto — "why, there
ain't no one as says I ain't the best shot hereabouts." He came slowly toward her. "Kin
you fire a pistol?"

"Give it me and let me try," said Meetah,
her eyes flashing as she held out her hand.

"Did yer ever see murder in an eye?" said
Bob, hoarsely laughing and turning to Dumfrey,
who still stood near the door.

"Hold up, Bob, and come away. You ain't
in good visitin' trim to-day," was the answer.

"Who says I ain't?" he retorted, suddenly
squaring himself. "No one can handle a six-
shooter like me."

He raised his revolver to take aim, and before
Meetah could think what he would do, he stood
beside her, his pistol pointed toward the crib.
"See how near I can come to the kid without
hittin'."

With a swift motion Meetah threw herself
forward, all her weight upon his raised arm ; but
too late : click went the trigger, the ball swerved
and whizzed by. Meetah's eyes, wide with
terror, were riveted upon the child. She rushed

across the room and caught it in her arms; a
cry escaped her, a cry of nervous relief as the
ball lay imbedded in the crib, and the startled
child was unhurt.

"Yer needn't be afraid," said Bob. "I was
just givin' an exhibition of my shootin'. Now,
if yer'll hold it in yer arms, up like, I'll knock
its eye out without so much as touchin' a hair
on yer head; but if yer will —"

He never finished the sentence. He was
seized from behind with a firm hand, and suddenly found himself outside the door. Gradually he awoke to the realization that he had
been ignominiously kicked out. He could see
Dumfrey running down the hill. With a terrible oath he turned to enter the house, but found
the door closed and bolted. Like a tiger that
has been denied its prey, he hungered to make
the man who had flung him forth his victim.
Softly he glided down the mountain path; he
could wait to spring. "But that —— fool who
kicked him out should feel what it was to pay
for his fun!" For a few moments he was so
entirely mastered by his animal nature, that his
rage blinded him as to whom it might be, — he
was glutting his imagination with the vengeance
he would wreak, — but it was an easy matter to
spot the man. Cautiously creeping back to the
house, he crawled along to the side window and,

peering in, saw Lorin Mooruck with the child in his arms, sitting near Meetah, whose back was toward the window. He drew his pistol out; it would be a fine thing to put a bullet in the back of her head; but as she leaned forward, put her hand upon Lorin's knee and looked up into his face, Bob McHenry's arm dropped. He seemed quivering with savage glee; he chuckled hoarsely to himself, and stealing away, muttered between his broken teeth, "I know a better way to bring yer round, my fine young squaw — a better way;" and so, skulking down the mountain side, he came upon his cowardly partner waiting for him behind a huge boulder.

He twitted and threatened him by turns for running from so small game as a lone Indian, then forgave him enough to reveal his fiendish plan. Together they talked it over, rolling from side to side with boisterous laughter. Dumfrey's explosive words were tinged with deep enjoyment as he ejaculated between bursts of hee-haws, "You're a rare one! you'll get both birds with one stroke!"

"You cannot remain here longer, Meetah," Lorin was saying. "I could scarce keep my fingers from that man's throat; but if I did violence to him, I knew every one in the village would be made to suffer. Death is too good for him; hell not bad enough. To think that *you* can be in danger from that fiend!"

"It is not so much that I am in danger," she answered. "I will come to no worse harm than death, if that be harm; and oh, it would! How could I give up our future! Why cannot we live like other people! We are hunted and hounded as though we were cursed. Do the people in the East know there are white savages? They talk of helping us. Oh, if I could but speak to the world and tell the truth!"

"We are so far away, they cannot realize our true life," he answered.

"But we have no chance to work out our lives. They border our villages with the depraved white people their crowded cities will not tolerate; and at last, when we refuse to submit to these border thieves, they think in the East — why, there are savages there, but they always picture them *red* savages. There is no one to tell our story. Do you think if I were to speak, any one would listen?"

"I do not know, Meetah; I think there are some prejudiced people who remember only the past. They would think you the only developed person out of your whole people."

"But look at Leena, at Natsee, at John Turner, Elmer, Francis, — why, no end of our friends who are as anxious as we — "

"I know," he interrupted; "but you could not take them with you. You could not dissolve deep-rooted prejudice in an instant; it must be gradual. If we had a surer faith that what we did was not altogether hopeless, we would do it better; more men and women in the village would take heart. Our people have lived here in peace for over sixty years; but if we are to be denied the right to our own homes and driven away by violence, we shall have to fight. People are so used to hear that we are driven from our homes, that it makes no impression upon them : they cannot picture what it means to us. If it were a different people in a foreign country who were thrust out, they would sympathize with them, raise money, offer them homes here, no matter how degraded they were ; but we, no matter how we strive to improve, they have no sympathy for us in this country; they think we are not human."

"But they were kind to me, Lorin," she said, softly rubbing her cheek against that of the cooing child, which had glanced up frightened into Lorin's face as he spoke, and held out its arms to her. "They cling to the picturesque, and fancy we are always riding wild horses, with feathers stuck in our hair. If they saw me in this common calico gown, saw me at the wash-tub, or teaching school, I know they would be provoked," she said, laughing. "But I do get very much out of patience, and sometimes," raising her earnest eyes to his, "sometimes I feel so strong in spirit, as if I could do so much for us all, and suddenly I imagine a sea of white, incredulous faces turned to mine — then, I am sick at heart. I feel that we are misunderstood by people willing to help us, if they could only realize that we are eager and willing to help ourselves; but the reports they hear are always of Indians who fight; one side only is shown; they do not know how for very home, life, wife, child, the Indian has been driven to fight. There are many people whose hearts are filled with good purpose. The false impression they have of us works us the greatest wrong. I saw it when I was East : all the people looked and wondered that I was an Indian, and yet had their ways and knowledge; half of them do not remember that through an Indian's exertion in lecturing, a great part of the money for Dartmouth College was raised. They are always amazed to see us educated."

"It is too late to turn back," Lorin answered. "We must advance. But the pity of it is that we have not yet learned the grasping tendency of the whites. I was trying to persuade old Samson to-day that the white man's God was full of love and compassion, but he said, 'I do

not believe it. The white man's God is money.
I pray to the Great Spirit, but the white man
prays to money — the silver dollar.' "

"I do not wonder at Samson's impression.
Perhaps it would be better if I only thought of
our lives, — yours and mine ; but all my life I
have been weighted with the sorrows of our
people."

"It is because you are a brave woman," he
answered, tenderly and proudly, "and never will
be content to live to yourself. Whatever you
do will be right, Meetah. If you go out to
make the world hear the truth, be sure my spirit
always will be near you. Nothing can part us ;
death itself would not forbid my love to reach
you, or yours to affect all my being." He arose,
and leaning back of her chair, touched her hair
with his lips. "I am sure you carry a blessing
with you wherever you go, whatever you do.
Meetah, if I should ever — "

"What was that, Lorin ? " cried Meetah,
starting up.

There was a slow rattling movement of the
kitchen door : both went out to see, and as
Lorin unfastened and opened wide the clap-
board door, Joseph and Hannah entered. Meetah
heaved a quick sigh of relief to find it was only
they ; a smile curved the corners of her mouth,
as she became conscious of her nervousness.

Hannah's face was radiant with smiles; Joseph looked solemn, but no longer troubled.

"We have the money!" Hannah exclaimed.

"The money!" ejaculated Meetah, with clouded brow.

"Well," said Hannah, "not exactly the money, but just as good. The Iroots, Hamptons, Johnsons, and others have said they would give the money to us that they would have given the lawyer if he had taken up the case against McHenry."

"But," interposed Meetah, "because of their sympathy they do not stop to think that you would be paying Bob McHenry for spoiling cornfields."

Hannah looked troubled and disappointed. Lorin felt sorry for her, and said, "Don't you see, Hannah, that what Meetah says is true? If you gave him the money that was to have been used to try the case against him, you would really be paying him for cheating you. Don't you see, Joseph, that by giving him the money, you will be acknowledging that your one cow destroyed his fields? Can't you see that it would be absurd? You ought not to give the man one cent. Let the matter rest awhile. Meetah will be safe at Mr. Tuscan's, and I will see if my good friend Mr. Harrold cannot get this thing straightened out: there certainly is some way. I will start to-night instead of to-morrow, and see Mr. Harrold in the morning. I am sure he will help us."

"Tell your friends we do not want the money," said Meetah, persuasively. "They were all too good to offer it. We will see if we are not in some way protected by the law."

"When you see Bob McHenry," said Moo ruck, turning to Joseph, "tell him I will settle all with him. Meetah will be at Mr. Tuscan's, and you will be safe here for a little time."

"Easy to say," Hannah replied dejectedly, as she threw off her shawl, and took the child from Meetah. "Fair words are easily said and easier forgotten. It is one thing to look at the sunshine, but one needs more heart to face the gloom. Bob McHenry is a crafty man, and we have no protection against him."

It took a great deal of patient showing before Joseph and Hannah could be made to see that they must not give McHenry money; as for the shooting, neither Lorin nor Meetah men-tioned it.

It was late in the afternoon when Meetah bade them good by, and with Lorin, who car-ried her little box, went to the Tuscans'.

After tea was over, Mr. Tuscan and his wife left Lorin and Meetah to visit alone, and when they returned from the evening service, they found Lorin still there. He arose in surprise as they entered. He was to leave that night, and yet the time had seemed. so short he had not dreamed how late it was.

Meetah followed him to the gate. The sadness of the lingering parting only enhanced the brightness of their future life when nothing would separate them.

At last Lorin was gone, and Meetah brooded alone in the darkness, miserably happy. "Ah!" she sighed, "these three days have passed like no others in my life — never to be lived again. Yet, if I try, my life will grow better,— our days may be more beautiful. I ought to be a noble woman with such happiness as this in my heart." Turning about, she entered the house with smiling face.

CHAPTER VII.

MR. HARROLD'S LETTER.

LORIN'S eyes were raised to the stars as he rode over the foot-hills at the base of the moun-tain, his whole being filled with the grandeur of the unalterable will and purpose of his Creator, the sublimity of space, the fathomless radiance above. The vast silence awed him ; he paused a moment, drinking in the glory of the whole. Then, in a rich, soul-vibrant voice, his spirit alive with adoration, he broke forth into the Te Deum Laudamus, and, as he wound on around the mountain slope, answering echoes followed him, the mountain's voice quivering with the ascending praise and exultation.

When Meetah awoke next morning and found herself in the Tuscans' home, she could not at first remember where she was; but soon she was up, helping the children dress, and after an early breakfast, hurried as usual to the school-house.

At night she came home tired but expectant, hoping for some word from Lorin. He would be at Crespy that morning, and certainly Pietro, the mail-carrier, who was his friend, would bring some message to her as he passed through the village on his way to Fort S——; but no letter came that day. Meetah sighed, smiled, and knew she had expected to hear too soon.

The next day, when she went to the store and asked for a letter, she was again disappointed, but the store-keeper gave her a letter for Mr. Tuscan. It was directed in a broad, clear hand, and bore the postmark of Crespy. Meetah's heart was aflutter as she walked along and gazed at the letter in curious wonder — it might have some message for her; but she laughed at her own impetuosity, and, handing it to Mr. Tuscan, flew away to her room to work out some difficult problem in arithmetic for the morrow's lesson. She wished to make sure she had not forgotten it; beside, it would serve to work off her nervous expectancy. Scarcely had she opened her book when Mr. Tuscan called from the bottom of the stairs. She hurried down and found him in the sitting-room.

"Take a chair, my dear girl," he said, spreading the letter out upon his knees, and readjusting his spectacles.

But Meetah stood waiting. Something in his voice startled her. He looked up over the brim of his spectacles, as she remained standing. Instantly her old habit of obedience came back;

she seated herself upon the edge of a chair opposite, and was silent with dread.

"This letter is from Mr. Harrold," Mr. Tuscan explained; "it is about Mooruck."

She did not speak.

He looked up at her. "Would you like to read it, my dear?"

"Thank you, yes." She eagerly held out her hand for it. The kind minister's troubled, gray eyes were fixed upon her face as she read : —

Town of Crespy.
Monday evening.

Dear Mr. Tuscan : —

I have often heard Lorin Mooruck speak of you, and know you will give him this message.

She looked up at the date. It was written Monday.

I do not direct the letter to him, because there is a good deal of double play hereabouts where an Indian is concerned. I fear he would never receive it. Will you kindly tell him that I expected him to-day.

Meetah caught her breath.

Tell him to come as soon as possible. Work is promised that only he can finish. I know some matter of importance has detained him, but tell him to start immediately, and you will greatly oblige,

Yours very truly,
Andrew Harrold.

She handed the letter back. " Mr. Balch goes to Crespy in to-night's stage," she gasped. " I will go too. Lorin is sick. We will find him somewhere on the road. Quick! Mr. Tuscan, get me some brandy, some linen, some food. Please send Henry to Mr. Balch to say that I will go too."

Before Mr. Tuscan could speak, she had left the room.

"This will never do," muttered the minister, shaking his head and calling for his wife Nancy, whose wise counsel helped him out of many difficulties. She appeared in the door-way, her hands covered with flour. After reading the letter she carefully wiped her hands, smoothed down her apron, and announced decidedly : "No biscuits for supper to-night! Of course she wants to go, — the most natural thing in the world, poor child! Go find your old satchel, Philip ; I will put the necessary things in it. It is in the garret somewhere, — on the top shelf, I think, beside those pamphlets. I will go and help Meetah, poor girl!" And she bustled off with motherly tenderness.

"Well!" Mr. Tuscan ejaculated, "they certainly take things in an odd way. I will not tell them what I think. Poor Meetah!" Dropping upon his knees he offered a prayer, asking with fervor that Lorin and Meetah might each be protected from all harm.

When he arose, his first thought was to see Mr. Balch. He entirely forgot about the satchel, the linen, brandy, and food; he opened the outer door and walked rapidly, with head bent, down the path, almost knocking down a woman in his haste.

"Oh! it is you, Hannah!"

"I suppose Meetah is in the house?" she asked.

"Yes; she is in the house," he answered slowly, taking time to think whether it would be best to tell Hannah about the letter or not. Then after due consideration he said:—

"Have you heard about Lorin?"

"Only that he was at Smike's Ranch at daylight Monday. You have heard from him since he got to Crespy, I suppose?"

"Who told you he was at Smike's Ranch? Did any one see him there?"

"Tomlinson told Joseph he saw him and spoke to him there."

"You had better go and tell Meetah," said Mr. Tuscan. "She had not even heard that much; we were afraid something had happened to him. Tell Meetah I want to see her too, will you?" and he followed Hannah into the house, and, while she found her way up stairs,

lay back in an easy-chair wondering what means
he had best use to prevent Meetah from starting
for Crespy.

He waited some time, revolving over and over
different means of persuasion that might have
effect upon her, yet she did not come. Over-
head he heard a treading to and fro, accompanied by the low voices of women; growing
impatient, he opened the door to call her, but
she was coming slowly down the stairs, followed
by Hannah, who passed swiftly across the room,
wishing him good-night as she closed the porch
door.

"I have been waiting for you," smiled Mr.
Tuscan, good-naturedly.   "Your sister has told
you the news?"

Meetah bowed her head.

"It is much better for you not to go: it
would be a useless journey. Lorin got to
Smike's Ranch all right, and in all probability
there is some mistake in Mr. Harrold's letter —
some error about the date. If he is in Crespy,
Mr. Harrold has seen him by this time. Wait
until to-morrow. It will be useless for you to
go, perfectly useless," he repeated, as she made
no reply and stood perfectly still, no trace of
excitement in either her face or manner. Somehow all his preconceived logic vanished; his sympathetic nature overcame all reasoning power,

his heart ached for her, and perhaps, after all, Mooruck had not reached Crespy. "It is almost time for the stage now," he continued, resolved to be prudent. "You are not ready, and it is best that you decided not to go."

"You have always been very good to me, Mr. Tuscan"—her soft eyes fixed upon his kindly face. "Until now I have always been glad to take your wise counsel; but now,—I think I know myself what is right now." She came toward him with both hands outstretched. "You will forgive me? I know you mean to be a good friend to us both, but you would not ask me to leave Lorin, dying, alone, in misery, without aid?"

"Well, well," he said, his eyes moist as he took her hands in one of his, softly stroking them with the other, "perhaps you are right; I do not dare to judge. I will go for the satchel, as Nancy said."

She detained him. "There is no need; Mrs. Tuscan found an old bag for me. My things are packed. I am all ready when I put on my bonnet and shawl."

"I will go and tell Mr. Balch, then. It behooves me to be active,"—with a smile,—"else I might break down, for you are so brave, dear girl!"

Her calmness distressed him more than tears.

"I shall be thankful if you will see Mr. Balch and say I would like to go with him — but one moment, please, until I tell you my plans. Hannah has gone to ask Elmer Stone to come too. He was going into Crespy the last of the week. Lorin rode a horse of his, and he is going to bring it home with him. He is going to visit Lorin. I thought he might start with me to-night; he has a pony I often ride. Hannah has gone to ask him to bring that too, so that after we reach Smike's Ranch we can go off the main road, over the mountains, and search for Lorin. He will likely bring John Turner with him, and they will ride with the stage until we reach the ranch. Then I will mount, and we will start off. I remember hearing Lorin say that a shorter road ran along the slope of the mountain ; he may have taken that. Hannah will see about some one to take my place in school, though whom, I cannot think."

"No matter, my dear ; don't worry about that ; I can easily get some one to fill your place. I have a man in my mind this very minute — he'll do first rate," said Mr. Tuscan cheerily, thinking of himself. "Now I will go and see our friend, Mr. Balch. I could not consign you to better hands. He is a fatherly man, has daughters of his own at home, and I am sure he will care for you."

Mrs. Tuscan tried in vain to persuade Meetah to take some food before the stage came.
When the rumbling stage drove up, Meetah, in
bonnet and shawl, with her bag in hand, was
waiting at the gate. Several people in the village had heard of her going, and a knot of men
and women had gathered to bid her good by
and God speed. •

She knelt with bowed head as an old man
with wrinkled face and long white hair feebly
raised his hands in blessing over her. He was
the oldest man in the village, and much rev-
erenced by the people : it was a good omen,
they whispered, that he was there to bless
Meetah.

Elmer Stone was there also, and called to
Meetah as the stage drove off, "I will be up
to you before the stage reaches the ranch : you
can trust me to be there when you need me."

She smiled sadly, waving her hand. She
knew well that Elmer would keep his word.

Over the creek and around the mountain they
rode in the coming dusk, Mr. Balch keeping
silent, for he knew Meetah was busy with
serious plans. The darkness fell, and still
they rode over creek and mountain, the little
rill of water coming back again and again for
the nineteenth time, till they left it and plunged
into a narrow ravine. The night grew apace,

the moon hid her light, and on they rode, dark
mountains rising on either side like huge mon-
sters. Meetah leaned far out, trying to catch
sight of the stars that unwillingly glimmered
amidst the passing clouds; then wearily throw-
ing herself back against the seat, she exclaimed:
"I wish I had my knitting, something, anything to do — anything but this terrible waiting
with hands folded. A thousand thoughts rush
through my mind, the last more horrible than
the first. What *do* you think could have happened to Lorin?"

Mr. Balch, appealed to in this passionate
manner, endeavored to imagine something to
detain Lorin, something with no evil following.
At last he said, "No doubt his horse has gone
lame, and he is obliged to walk."

"Ah! yes," Meetah answered slowly; "if it
only were that, but — " then she tightened her
lips and became silent.

As the morning dawned, they wound around the
curved mountain road, down into a deep cañon,
and out upon an open plain; stray cattle grazing here and there told of some habitation near.

Meetah leaned far out of the stage, glancing
back to see if Elmer Stone and his friends were
coming; but no one followed them.

"You think they will come in time, do you?"
Mr. Balch asked anxiously.

"Yes, I am sure Elmer will come. He will be in time. I cannot bear to think I might have to wait at the ranch—I could not. If they are not there when we arrive, I shall go on alone, on foot. I cannot wait to see where Lorin is and what has happened."

"If they are not there, I shall go on with you," Mr. Balch said decidedly. "I presume they could accommodate me at the ranch until to-morrow."

"I would not have you wait," Meetah interposed. "I am not afraid to go alone, but Elmer promised to bring the pony for me. I am sure he will come. They were not to leave until midnight; and if they took the road over the mountain, they ought to come out on this plain somewhere near here, as that path joins this road. They will surely come."

She relapsed into silence; but as the wheels revolved, her thoughts kept time: "The horses are so slow — so slow — so slow. Drive faster, faster, faster! O God! keep him safe from harm! If the driver would let me urge the horses once, just once. If they would go faster, faster, faster!"

Suddenly behind them arose a cloud of dust; they could see the ranch in the distance, — a low, rambling, one-storied dwelling made of mud and stones. The ranch was now only a quarter of a mile away; cattle were grazing near the road; goats, watched by a faithful shepherd dog, stopped nibbling and raised their bearded chins and staring eyes, as the creaking stage, with its white, dust-covered horses, drew near. Still nearer came the cloud of dust; Meetah looked out. "Thank God, they have come at last!" she said reverently, but at that moment shots struck the stage. One of the horses plunged, reared, and fell; the stage stopped with a jerk. The air was filled with the sound of cries and whizzing bullets.

Mr. Balch, in excitement, anger, and surprise, thought, "This is treachery — so much for an Indian's promise!"

But Meetah heard Elmer's voice above all the din. "Quick! It is the people at the ranch; a flag of truce!"

She snatched part of a sheet from her bag, that was meant for bandages. Seizing Mr. Balch's umbrella, she tied one end to it, and sprang out amidst the shots and cries.

CHAPTER VIII.

THE LIGHT STRUCK OUT.

THE people at the ranch, seeing the white flag, suspended hostilities. Elmer Stone urged his pony toward Meetah, and leaning over, took the flag from her trembling hand, as he murmured, "Bravely done," and galloped on toward the ranch.

Two of his friends came forward to help the stage driver, who was striving to remove the harness from the dead horse; a third bent over the wounded form of a comrade. Meetah hastened to him. With Mr. Balch as assistant, she succeeded in binding the wounded arm of young Wahsoo; she gave him some brandy from the flask in her bag, and then left his friend to care for him while she and Mr. Balch walked quickly toward the ranch.

An excited group crowded about the door of the long, low, mud-colored building. In their midst, his back toward Meetah Tocare and the Eastern gentleman, was Elmer Stone demanding an explanation. Back in the hall, near the door, were the shrinking forms and white faces of the women. The question, in Meetah's eyes and on her lips, was for Lorin, but she controlled her impatience and waited.

"I see no excuse for your firing upon us as though we were a pack of hungry wolves," Elmer was saying. "What were you afraid of?"

"That's just it. We seen a lot of Injuns swoopin' down on us, and thout we'd show fight."

"Smike, you'd best make a clean breast of it," said one of the men, nudging him; "no one's goin' to take your scalp."

Smike looked cautiously about, as though an assassin lurked near, and lowering his voice, said: "The truth of it is, we thout you'd come down to burn th' ranch and murder every mother's son of us. We thout you'd come for revenge. That's the whole of it;" spreading his hands as though having laid bare his soul.

"That's a queer story," said Elmer Stone; "revenge for what?"

Smike glanced around keenly at his own men and answered: "We heard of a row a few miles beyond, down by th' creek, between some whites an' some of the men from your village. You might ride on an' see if you rec'nize any of 'em. We thout mebbe you might toss the blame on us. We'd nothin' to do with it. We seen you comin' on in the dust, an' thout there was more

on you. I'm sorry 'bout the firin', but blessed if
I could a held th' men back."

While he spoke, Elmer's quick eye glanced
into the hall where the women were huddled
together. He noticed two strapped trunks, and
near them, shawls and bags: the women wore
bonnets.

"Why are the women going to leave the
ranch?" he asked suddenly. "They were evi-
dently going on this stage. You have killed
the horse: unless you put one in its stead they
will have to wait." Fixing his clear, penetrative
gaze upon Smike, he continued: "We will not
remain much longer waiting for the truth. You
have not told it. Why are the women to leave?
and why do you persist in lying? As I rode up,
I saw that cream-colored mare over there: this is
not the first time I have seen that animal. You
might as well tell the truth now, and here." He
dismounted, and holding his pony by the bridle,
walked up and faced Smike.

As he spoke, each one in the group glanced at
the mare, grazing at the end of its lariat rope,
but neither Meetah nor Mr. Balch understood
the reference.

"I'm not afraid to tell th' story if you want
it," blurted out Smike, who was in truth a good
fellow, but had been until now inventing tales,
that the women might have time to get off. It

was evident that Elmer Stone was no hostile; the truth might as well be told.

"Monday mornin' come along a man from your village, an' wanted breakfast here. Of course you know he rode that there cream mare."

Meetah's cheeks paled, her lips parted, her eyes glowed.

"He carried a tony rifle with him." .

Yes; Meetah remembered the beautiful initials he had carved upon the butt.

"He was standin' right along-side of th' buildin', leanin' on his rifle like, waitin' for his grub, when up rides two settlers. I could spot either one of th' rough cowards. I saw 'em after; only th' women was here then. One on 'em, th' biggest, drops off his horse, comes up to the Injun an' says, 'Le' me have that gun!' My old woman told me the Injun says, 'No,' and somethin' 'bout squarin' accounts. With that the man calls out, 'Dumfrey, jump off an' take it.' T'other fellow jumps from his horse and reaches for the rifle. Back steps the Injun. T'other man knocks the Injun down from behind; the Injun struggles, but th' man with the rifle springs forward and knocks the Injun over th' head. He fell in the doorway there. The women begged the men not to murder him; his tribe would come and kill us; but they dragged him, half senseless as he was, and killed him. We buried him yonder on the plain."

An agonized shriek pierced the air, making the men and women shiver. Meetah, wild-eyed and with terrible force, staggered toward the man, and grasping him by the arms, cried out, "The truth! Is that the truth?"

He started back, terror-stricken, gasping, as he tried to shake himself free, "Take her off! She is mad!"

Elmer turned upon Mr. Balch. "Had you no mercy, no pity, to bring her here?"

As he spoke, Meetah's arms fell. "You do not believe it is true," she said, raising her tortured face to him.

"I fear something terrible has happened," he said in an awed, solemn voice.

She turned slowly from one face to another in the silent group, with eyes that seemed to have lost their sight; then her gaze rested upon Elmer Stone. She pointed her finger at him, saying, in a rapid, smothered voice, "You know Lorin. Take me to him."

"Heaven knows I would if I could. Thank God! she does not realize what has happened."

"The grave is over yonder," jerked out Smike, pointing over on the plain.

"Come!" and Meetah wildly grasped at Elmer's arm. "Come! He needs me."

Elmer handed the reins of his pony to a man near. The men and women, who had crowded around, fell back in awed silence. Meetah followed close upon Smike's footsteps, as he led the way, her arms crossed beneath the back of her head, her eyes upon the ground as though searching for something lost. Elmer,·in pain and sorrow, walked near her, Mr. Balch following. In the background were the men and women, uncertain whether to come or to remain where they were.

Upon the broad prairie, surrounded by rugged mountains, lay a little mound of newly turned earth. About it grouped the four peo· ple, the men with heads uncovered, Meetah in the same strange position, her eyes upon the dark mound.

Suddenly she loosened her arms, looked up with wide, dark-lined eyes, and in a voice never to be forgotten, asked, " Will you not leave me? It is mine. Leave me to my own." Her eyes fell, her lips trembled; and as they turned away, she cast herself upon the ground, moaning piteously.

The three men stood at a distance beneath a clump of young trees, Elmer Stone with prayers and entreaties begging them to go away and leave Meetah to herself; he would watch over her from a distance. " Some people might faint with grief, but her sorrow is too deep for that."

Finally they left him watching. He strove painfully to realize her grief, to put himself in perfect sympathy with her.

Meetah's mind aroused itself to a dim consciousness of darkness closing in upon every side. She could not escape it; she might fight to the death, but this darkness would choke her. She could never wake in light again. She might dig deep into the earth, but this darkness would surround her. What to do! Face it, stifle it, yet would it arise and envelop her. A moment ago Lorin was with her — in a breath he was gone, annihilated. It took but a moment. Something had happened. They were never again to be together. She was left alone in a cold, vast space where he would never come. Why should a moment drag all light from a life? a moment, such a little thing, why should it be a gulf to divide happiness from eternity? Happiness — eternity — what were they? She laughed shrilly. What was either? No one could tell. People always differed over nothing; there was neither. She half raised herself upon her hands; her shawl and bonnet had fallen off. Why, the sun was shining! It was round and bright — was that God?

Her eyes fell upon the earth. "That damp

mound, what is it?" she muttered. "Ah, Lorin's
statue! that is it; they are trying to hide it.
They have buried it; they are afraid people
will see. They fear he will be great. Ha-ha!
ha-ha! He shall! He shall! I will uncover it.
Lorin, never fear; you *shall* be great!"

With tugging and hasty breathing, she dug
in the wet clay, clawing handfuls of the earth
away.

Elmer Stone, hearing the insane laughter,
hastened to her, but not until the ghastly form
of Lorin Mooruck lay half uncovered, as she
bent above, crooning a soft lullaby.

Horrified and amazed, he knew that much
depended upon his self-command.

"What are you doing?" he said sternly.

She started and looked up at him with a
blank stare.

"Come, get up. You are going to Crespy."
He held out his hands to her. "Come; we are
going to Crespy."

Slowly a light seemed to dawn in her bewildered face; she half arose, then turned to look:
suddenly, with a terrible cry, she seemed to
realize what was before her. She got hastily
upon her feet. "They made him suffer. Revenge! that is all that is left." She paused,
turned slowly backward, and with arms outstretched, cried, "Lorin, Lorin, come back to

me. O God! I cannot bear it! Lorin! Lorin!"
She took one step forward and fell heavily.

* * * * * * *

The sun was shining, the birds were singing,
and the yellow stage, drawn by a white horse
and a small cream-colored mare, came rattling
over the prairie on its way to the village of
Natsee : in it were two well-dressed men from
Maine. The younger was hastily making notes
as they jolted along, He was, for the time, a
special correspondent for a New York weekly.

The older man, a senator, had come out to
this unknown country for new scenes and sights,
to rest his mind and exercise his body, after a
busy city life.

"Hollo!" said the younger, as the plain disappeared, and they plunged into a ravine, "what
is that curious object over there? No. You
are looking the wrong way ; the other side of
the ravine — something jogging along. Couldn't
be a buffalo all by himself."

"Possibly ; I hardly think so," replied the
senator. "Some curious phenomena of the
West. I see you have your pencil ready."

"Yes," laughed the younger. "Down she
goes when we get nearer."

An hour afterwards he wrote : "Five Indians
on the mountain path — one leading six horses,
using his left hand — stolid, well-knit fellows.

Use ponies only in war; when travelling save the ponies' muscle and waste their own. Indians with close-cut hair and civilized dress! Four of them carrying a box — weight heavy; two poles attached to box, one on either side."

"There, there! now we're near enough to speak. ·I say, driver, driver! Give you a dollar to stop ten minutes! Hope they'll pay well for this article." The horses are pulled up; the stage stops.

"Hollo there!" cries the enthusiast; then *sotto voce*, "Don't suppose they know a word of English."

The men stopped; the one following with the ponies also stood still.

"Where are you bound for?"

Elmer Stone answered, "For the village of Natsee." The four men slowly lowered their burden, resting it upon the ground.

"You speak English! Is that the way you carry freight?" asked the correspondent, pencil in hand.

Elmer Stone did not answer; but Wahsoo, who was leading the ponies, spoke in a hushed voice: "It is the body of our friend, Lorin Mooruck."

"Ah!" the correspondent paused, then asked, "You have his horse with you? Was it an accident?"

Elmer pointed to one of the horses drawing the stage : "That was the horse he rode. No accident : he was killed in a brutal manner by two white men who attacked him in the presence of some helpless women."

"Why did they kill him?"

"It is a sport of some white men here, an amusement."

"But why do you carry him that way? why not bury him at home?"

Elmer turned his deep eyes upon the questioner. "He has gone to his Home. We are taking the shell back to the place of his childhood."

Surprised at the answer, the correspondent turned to his friend, "Queer!"—then to Elmer, "Don't suppose you know that a bill has passed Congress, making you citizens of these United States; under certain conditions, though."

"I have heard," was the laconic answer.

"Your land is to be apportioned to individuals; after that you are citizens."

"Each of us has his patch of land now, marked off and fenced. Under your law we cannot rent our land — it would be of no use then to us who work in the lumber mills and have no time for farming, or to the men who can the salmon ; beside, one hundred and sixty acres could not be found together for a farm —

we live among the mountains; as for grazing, few of us have enough cattle to need much land for that. Your law is good for some Indians, but not for us. All white cities have not the same laws, neither will one law be good for all Indian villages — make it to suit different cases. But we want courts, we want law. *He* was a citizen," pointing to the rough box upon the ground, "subject to your laws. Let us see if he will be protected by them."

It was rather embarrassing to the correspondent, who had come out to teach the Indian, to find him talking about law and the practical use of a bill approved by the educated men of the nation who were interested in the aboriginal's welfare; but swallowing his chagrin, he asked, "What do you mean by the law protecting him? He is dead."

"Yes, murdered without cause by a white settler, a citizen. A coward striking out the life of a pure, noble soul. We will see what the law does. The white man comes here and preaches God and right; beside him come other white men sacrificing the lives of our women and children. There is a flag, it is said, to protect those under it; but us, you put outside of it. A week ago your citizens offered a reward for the scalp of any one of us. In our village is law and order, but outside of it, here, lawless-

ness and death reign. You talk of the law;
what use is it unless you can enforce it? Your
law is bought and sold here. We pay no tax;
therefore your men hold us not worth the law.
You wish us to become part of the Republic.
You legislate; even this law you speak of, what
is it unless properly carried out? You form
laws for our good; at the same time you allow
border men to take law into their own hands.
There are others beside philanthropists who
form laws and carry them out." He pointed to
the rough coffin with tragic intensity. "There
is their answer. Come among us if you would
have the right done. You try to help us from
too long a distance. Unless you are ready to
come and see your good plans carried out, you
merely dream about us, — think of us as a people unwilling for anything but a forest life. Do
not come to the village and see a poor, striving,
hard-working mass; people who love, hope,
weep, laugh, and die. Go back to the East,
think you have made good laws, and there is an
end of wrong; else put the fire of your soul
into the work, and bring us your law to be carried out, your courts where justice is supreme.
Bring us your civil protection. Make laws for
our welfare, but enforce them."

The newspaper correspondent felt rebuffed.
He had not expected to meet an Indian as a

man to respect. He imagined them helpless, dependent ; he meant to sympathize with them.

The Indians took up their burden. The stage rumbled on, while the eager young man from Maine dropped his head forward, lost in thought, and the older man murmured : —

"After all, he is right. Making a good law is but one step for the right ; unless one sees it properly carried out, it were better not made. Some people will let their interest cease when a good law comes into view. They think all has been done ; they stop at the most important point, — that of seeing it put into practice. A man is a man be he Indian or white ; God created each, and I hardly believe one was made to have dominion over another. Grant you, intellect is a power ; yet would I rather be an Egyptian mummy than a man all thought and no feeling." He paused ; he was having the conversation all to himself ; the correspondent was leaning over his note-book with pencil flying along the page.

CHAPTER IX.

THE LITTLE WHITE CROSS ON THE CLIFF.

THE people at the ranch were very good to Meetah. The women respected and were sorry for her; one of the women offered the use of her room, when they carried Meetah in, and there she was laid.

She gradually awoke to the darkness and despair of consciousness. She arose, and asked to be left alone. The woman quietly withdrew. She sat by the closed window, alone in the strange room. She pressed her fingers to her tearless eyes. Nothing could shut out the past; nothing could ward off the future.

In a desperate moment she had thought to end her own life; but that would only be putting her further away from Lorin : a criminal might never go where he was.

Anything would have been easier to bear than the thought that Lorin had suffered at the hands of murderers. If he had died of some terrible disease she might have thought it one of the plans in the all-wise Providence, but she

could never think such a violent death as his
the result of any Supreme Will.

She arose, shuddering. What was her own
grief; her own loss? They would press their
claims always; but Lorin's future, Lorin's life,
cut off, — Lorin's dreams ended here, and by
whom? Lorin an unwilling, defenceless victim,
Lorin struck down —

She rushed from the room. It was not too
late, the stage had not gone. They were trying
to master the cream-colored mare; they had
been hours trying to harness it.

Elmer Stone stood aloof, his hands shading
his eyes; Meetah glided to him.

"You will take Lorin back to the mountains
he loved? Do you remember the cliff, — the
place where Lorin loved to dream? — there."

She turned away; he understood what she
meant.

Elmer put out his hand. "And you? Where
are you going?" His voice was husky.

"For justice; if not, then revenge. Mr.
Harrold will help me. I shall go to him. I
shall not believe there is a God in heaven
if —"

"If what, Meetah?"

"Oh! I do not know. Do not ask me —"
Her face worked painfully as she turned away.

Mr. Harrold wondered and waited for Lorin

three days, and neither sight of him nor word. On the morning of the fourth day, as he sat beside his log fire, in the sitting-room, still wondering about Lorin, his door burst open, — a woman with haggard eyes and wan features stood upon the threshold.

"You did not hear my knock, and I could not wait. O Mr. Harrold, help me! Lorin is dead. Killed by two white men — murdered!" Then she stood staring before her. Suddenly: "On a lonely plain I found him, dead." Eagerly: "Have you seen him? Have you seen Lorin? Tell me, tell me, for I am Meetah Tocare."

She put her hands to her forehead, then with a puzzled look: "This is Mr. Harrold, I believe? I am Meetah Tocare. Have I told you about Lorin? — I am very weary. I do not believe I know what I say, I —." She paused, and in a hushed voice said, "He told me of this room. Oh, you were so good, so kind to him! Be good to me. Help me —."

Mr. Harrold could not doubt the horrible truth. All that Lorin had said of Meetah came back to him. Without a word he led her to an easy-chair, and, going to the cupboard, brought a glass of wine and put it to her lips. She drank it, and, leaning back her head wearily, closed her eyes. He stood a moment gazing at her. He

could not overcome the chilliness creeping
through his nerves.

Softly opening the hall door, he called his wife,
she who, as Miss Slater, had first directed his
attention to Lorin Mooruck. He spoke to her
hurriedly in the hall. She came into the room
and knelt by Meetah's side, taking the long,
slender hands of the Indian girl in hers. She
tenderly stroked them, while the hot tears rolled
down her cheeks at sight of Meetah's face.

At her touch, Meetah unclosed her eyes,
looking long and earnestly at her: "Yes, Lorin
spoke of you, too. You were good to him."
She leaned forward and lightly touched Mrs.
Harrold's cheek with the tip of her finger.
"Tears! You will help me, too, then."

She turned her face to the artist. "There
was a statue — you will let me see it." She
arose, steadied herself by the chair, refusing
assistance.

"Is it not better for you to rest, — to —" Mr.
Harrold paused.

"Me rest? me rest?" She shook her head
slowly. "No; no more rest for me; never
again."

He left her in the studio and turned silently
away, but not before he saw her start, catch
her breath, her hand to her heart, pause, then
fling herself upon her knees, her lips to the cold

marble, her arms thrown protectingly around it, while her whole form shook with convulsive sobs.

"Poor thing, poor thing! Don't you think we had better take her away?" said Mrs. Harrold, raising her tear-stained cheeks to her husband, as they heard the heart-bursting sobs.

"No," he said taking her hands in his; "no, Madge; these are probably the first tears the poor heart has shed." His voice trembled.

She laid her head against his breast. "Our happiness seems wicked in the face of grief like that. Tell me, is it because we are white and they are Indian, is that the reason it all happened? Isn't a man a *man*, no matter about the race? Is a heart and soul of no account?"

"I do not know," he answered. "God forbid that this wrong should be laid at our door, that we should forget the soul, forget manhood, right, and justice."

The manner of Lorin's death was very indistinct in the mind of Mr. Harrold and his wife, until Mr. Balch came and explained all to them.

Great anger was mixed with the artist's sorrow at loss of his friend. He swore by all holy things to help Meetah Tocare. He, too, cried, "If not justice, then revenge;" but first he would compel the law.

Mrs. Harrold proved a friend to Meetah; a sister could not have been more deferential or

thoughtful to such grief. Meetah remained the
Harrolds' guest for many days; looking up the
law, going with Mr. Harrold to first this one and
then that, endeavoring in all ways to urge the
law to mete out justice to Bob McHenry and
Dumfrey, of whom they had sufficient evidence
that they were the murderers.

Meetah spent much time in the studio, sitting
silently, her eyes on Mr. Harrold's work, or else
deep in dreaminess gazing at nothing. She
loved the place because there Lorin had begun
to realize his dreams.

One day as she stood beside Lorin's half-
finished statue, her fingers caressingly upon
the marble, she looked up at the artist, with
dreamy eyes and the shadow of a smile about
her lips, asking with hesitation, " Would it be
possible — do you think I could ever learn to do
as Lorin did ? Do you think with years of per-
severance and work, I could ever go on with this
— his work ? "

Mr. Harrold shook his head : " I am afraid not ;
no one but Lorin could finish that."

" It is like my life," she murmured, " half
done — half in the rough. The tools are dropped;
it will never be finished as was meant."

Mrs. Harrold dropped her white sewing : "Ah,
Meetah, you have that within you which is im-
mortal, that which is meant to be beautiful,

never to die. The statue's master is gone, the spirit is dead. Your Master lives always, His spirit lives in you. You will go on emerging ; heart-break and bitter sorrow are oftenest the tools with which His work is perfected."

Meetah's eyes flashed up at her ; then the tears filled them. She came to her, pressed her hand : "Thank you, my sister. You have given me a new thought." She passed silently from the room, her head bent.

Mrs. Harrold heaved a sigh as her eyes followed the girlish form. "I do not want her to give up her young life," she said, turning to her husband, "in endless rebellion. There is much useful work for her to do in the world; she has a strong influence, a fine mind, and what is more, a sympathetic heart. She is a help to all who know her ; there are many weary ones for her to help. Who knows, that might have been her mission,— to taste the bitter dregs so that she might be able to administer comfort to others."

"A very sad life, at best," the artist answered. "I think she might have helped others quite as much, if Lorin had not been brutally murdered."

At last Bob McHenry was arrested with the rifle in his hand. There could be no mistake, for the initials L. M. were wondrously carved upon the butt.

Dumfrey had fled the country, the sheriff

advising him to do so, until the excitement
should have died out.

The testimony of Smike, and that of the
women, established Bob McHenry's and his
accomplice's guilt beyond a doubt. After the
testimony and the examination, six thousand
dollars bail was accepted, and the murderer
released.

Meetah left the court-room in feverish excitement; she was ready to return to the village
now that the law was in operation; but Mr. Harrold, who lingered behind, saw the murderer, with
the judge, cross the street and enter a saloon.
He followed them, and was in time to hear the
judge order two drinks, and raising the glass to
his lips say, "Here's to you, Bob, hoping you'll
come through the business A, No. 1. It'ud
be best for you to skip the country, till this
Indian girl's friends cool off. The Indians'll
have to get out of the way soon; they'll object,
but we wont have any foolin'. We'll soon settle
the red-skins!"

When Mr. Harrold bade good by to Meetah,
the next morning, he had not the courage to tell
her that he believed Bob McHenry would go
unpunished.

Meetah was back among her friends, — those
who had loved Lorin and been proud of him.
They gathered about her, and she told them of

his statues. She left Mr. Tuscan to tell how far the law had gone. Some of the young men threatened to shoot either Dumfrey or Bob McHenry on sight; but Mr. Tuscan exerted all the influence he possessed among them, and they promised to await the course of the law.

The children very seldom walk from the school-house with Meetah now; she asks to be left alone, and sits there at her desk for hours, her head buried in her hands.

Every day she walks to the cliff. Where she and Lorin sat of yore stands a little white cross at the head of a grave.

This evening, as she sits there in the twilight, a horseman gallops up to Mr. Tuscan's door; it is Wahsoo with a message from Mr. Harrold. His news is soon told. A new trial had been given Bob McHenry, and to-day he had been proven innocent.

Little does Meetah dream of the word that awaits her, when she goes home to Hannah this night. She sits thinking of Mrs. Harrold's last letter, wherein she urges her to go East and lecture; to tell the people of Lorin; to show what education has done; to picture the village and the public spirit and ambition of both men and women; to prove that "a man's a man for a' that." Suddenly Lorin's words came to her, — those he spoke that Sunday when they together waited for Hannah and Joseph, the day she went to live with Mr. Tuscan; the air seems vibrant with them : —

"If you go out to make the world hear the truth, I will always be near you. My spirit shall help you."

She sits gazing at the mountains that are softened by the evening's shadow, her arm thrown over the grave. A rim of rosy light quivers in the blue above, then gives place to gray clouds growing darker and darker, until they envelop Meetah Tocare and shut her from our sight.

THREE MEN OF WALLOWA.

—◦o°◦°◦o—

IN the far distance, snow-capped mountains;
nearer, billowy, purple-hued hills; yet nearer,
a faint touch of green upon the hills, and at
their feet a valley, through which winds a
limpid stream.

The rudely built houses scattered over the
emerald vale are owned by warm-hearted men
and women; people who once owned the land
on which they lived, but who have been forced,
step by step, to yield to a Superior Power; a
Power that permits them to remain here a little
while, then jostles them aside, their labor lost,
their homes taken from them, to make room for
people from foreign lands.

It is a peaceful village to-night. The sun
sheds his rich light over hill and valley, as he
sinks beyond the mountain's crest.

The bare, square building across the field is
closed. Teachers and pupils have gone home
to rest. The herd has wound around the hill
and down the valley, and the bars of the corral
have been closed for the night. The tired

gleaners have left the field, but only as the sun
sank, men and women both wending their way
to the different log dwellings ; the men in coarse
working-dress, the women in worn calicoes.
Soon, before the homes of many is built the
evening fire.

From pine boughs and burning spruce the
flames leap high, often disclosing the family
circle around, who while the hours of the
short evening away with weird tale or merry
song.

The more studious are within the houses,
poring over the lessons for to-morrow, old and
young learning to read and write.

In among the trees there, a little to the right
of the limpid stream, is the home of Lapwar.
He and Medina, his wife, are within the house,
talking with serious air. The child they call
Bright Eyes has dropped asleep, the tired head
upon her mother's lap. On the door-step sits
the elder daughter, her back towards the room,
but her dark features lighted up by the fire that
splutters and spurts before the door-way ; it
brings into bold relief her straight nose and
strong chin, and glints along the heavy braids of
her dark hair that fall on either side of her narrow, sloping shoulders.

Her unconscious grace has won for her the
name of Bending Willow, and many are the

young men who long for her favor; among them is Creekie.

He has been jeered and laughed at for his bashful awkwardness. He may be in the midst of a village crowd, but utterly unconscious that any one is there, save Bending Willow. He wins at the races, he wins at the games, but only for the smile of Bending Willow.

To-night, he has come to tell her of his love. He is half concealed by the trees at the stream's edge, as he watches the firelight flicker across her face. There is a serious dream-look about her eyes as the uneven flames compel her gaze ; she in the light and warmth, Creekie shivering beside the stream.

They say he is brave in all save love. He plunges boldly forward, the branches crackle under his feet, he has an air of shy determination as he goes toward the girl, but suddenly she raises her head and listens. She has heard his foot-step ? No. Creekie cowers back to the stream as he sees the glad expectancy of her face, the love-light in her eyes, the smile about her lips, the joyous quivering of her form as, leaping from the steps, she shyly greets White Swan, the tall, careless son of Chief Sawyer.

Creekie watches them only a moment, then he slinks back to the shadow of the trees ; no one sees him, no one knows he has been there ; he

has read his fate, but in the smile of Bending
Willow. The tall trees, by the water's edge,
bend back to let him pass. Alone midst the
trees in the darkness, alone with his heart's sorrow, alone through the long hours of the night
he wrestles and prays.

A few years since he might have sought to
appease the wrath of some evil spirit; but
to-night he seeks the Great Father of us all.
Poor Creekie has always been favored until
now; the same blind rebellion that comes to
each of us, at times, comes to the bewildered
Indian; the same heavy curtain that shuts out
all light from us, at times, falls for him; were
there no thunder-clouds, no lightning would
illumine the distance.

"Faith in the darkness for all things," thinks
Creekie, "save such a sorrow as mine." But
here must be endurance for those whose love
is selfish; happiness for those whose sorrow is
drowned in the sight of the beloved one's joy.
Creekie's first thought was for himself, but, before the night wore away, his heart had righted
and his thought was for the happiness of Bending Willow, or Suzette, as he loved to call her.
He could always be near her, her happiness
would content him. But there rose a bitter
feeling in his heart towards White Swan. The
son of Sawyer was learned, he had been away

three years at school, he knew more than most men in the village.

Suzette had known White Swan but a short time, while Creekie she had known always; as children they had gone over together to the mission to learn and play, —it was the missionary's wife who had given her the name of Suzette, but that was long since.

The missionary had taught them the sweet hymns that rose at morning and at evening from the valley; but a great sorrow had come upon them,— Creekie shuddered when he thought of it; the Indian had not forgotten it, neither had the white man.

Some years ago a terrible disease broke out among the Indians; there was a death each day, sometimes two, sometimes three, — nothing seemed to stop the scourge; mothers watched their suffering children die, children their fathers, husbands their wives. Again and again did they seek their "medicine-man": he always gave them the same answer: "The squaw is dying, the papoose wails like the wind in the trees, the warrior is dead. The Red Man must live. The pale-faces walk among us. The pale-faces must go. The pale-faces must die that the Red Man may live." Always the same answer. Sorrowfully, slowly, the Indians went back to their sick and dying, solemnly they

buried their dead. Then one of the chiefs
went to the missionary and begged him to leave
them, saying : "In a little while you may return." But the missionary smiled, and would
not go. Then the Indian told him of the strong
influence the medicine-man exerted over the
tribe, and that some of the younger members of
the tribe firmly believed that he had brought
this plague upon them. The chief could not
restrain them much longer ; they would not sit
quietly by and see their people die. "My hands
and those of my people are free from the white
man's blood. We have protected the white
man against other Indians. We have always
been the white man's friend, but you must depart from us now. One hand is stretched out
in friendship — in the other there is the toma-
hawk."

The missionary smiled at fear. His friends
begged him to leave ; some of the Indians even
went to his distant friends and asked them to
persuade him to go, but he would not listen to
them.

One night, as he passed through the village,
an arrow whizzed towards him. No one knew
who sent the death-dart. There was a crazed
young man in the village who had lost both
wife and child that day, — perhaps it was he.

The Indians sought revenge, so also did the

white man, and before the summer was over war
and desolation swept through the valley.

Years had passed since then ; the Indians had
lost more than the whites. Whom shall we
blame, the superstitious Indian, or the reckless
missionary ? The Indians had warned him to
depart, only for a little time, while the tribe
were crazed with grief and swayed by the words
of their medicine-man.

Witches were burned in Massachusetts when
we had reached a much higher state of civilization than the Indians in this village. We yet
hold an entire tribe responsible for the action of
one or two men ; " a poor law that will not work
both ways," yet there are brawls and murders,
almost nightly, in Western and Southern villages,
where the murderers are not even brought to
justice, much less the whole village punished for
the crime of an individual member. I do not excuse the Indian. I condemn the white man's
law that protects the criminal, while refusing
the law to the Indian.

The morning sun rose brightly over the valley, and with it rose a sweet hymn from the
Indian village. As the sound died away, Lapwar was followed into the house by his wife and
daughters.

Seating themselves before the morning meal,
Lapwar bent his head to ask a blessing, then

served his wife and daughters. It was a merry meal, with much laughter and joking, but, as Medina followed her husband to the door, he bade her good-by, with sad eyes, saying, "My heart is like the clods I go to break, heavy"; and Medina can give him no cheery reply, their conversation of last night still weighing heavily upon her.

The white people beyond their village have taunted them of late, the settlers have encroached upon their grounds, some of their cattle have been stolen and branded by these settlers. Chief Sawyer has been twice to see about it; he has been told no one can prove who stole the cattle. "But," he urged, "I can point out one, one that belongs to Lapwar. Bending Willow made a pet of it. It is tame as a doe."

"But there is no use in your appearing against a white man in court; it can't be done; the jury will acquit him."

It was only true. What Western jury would agree in finding a white man guilty who had stolen from an Indian? A Pole, an Irishman, a Swede, a German, a negro, has the protection of the law, but an American Indian is helpless. He has no redress save that of war.

But this morning, as the men were working in the fields, word passed from one to the other that the Great Chief, the Governor of the Territory, had come to visit them. At last there was hope. He would see their wheat-fields, their corn, their vegetables, their school-house, their cattle ; he would see that they were trying "to walk in the white man's road"; he would help them to make their village still better; he would punish the men who took their homes, who ran off their stock; at last, justice had come to their village.

The Governor was a man recently appointed ; his object in coming here was to gain popularity with the people of the Territory. He and his companions came to Sawyer's house. The chief was working in the field ; one of his children ran to tell him. He came up smiling, his child upon his shoulder ; then, gently putting the child upon the ground, he held out his hand and welcomed the Governor; he was filled with joy at sight of him, he was honored by the visit. The Governor and his aide entered the house of Sawyer, ate of his bread, but, when they went forth, a line of soldiers stood in front of the house. Sawyer's eyes flashed and he darted a hasty glance at the Governor, then drew himself to his full height, folded his arms, and waited for Governor Lanigan to speak.

"My friend," said the Governor, smiling blandly, "perhaps you remember an affair that took place near here not many years ago, — the

massacre of the missionary. That massacre
brought on a great war in which many people
were killed. I represent your Father at Washington, and come here to demand the surrender
of those concerned in this horrible deed." He
paused, looked at the armed men, then at the
solitary Indian, and smiled.

"I have heard what you have to say," replied
Sawyer. "I knew the missionary and loved
him as a brother, but my whole tribe are not responsible for his death. We warned him many
times to leave, but he would not. I could no
longer restrain my young men who were wild
with grief. They did not wish to kill him.
They begged him many times to leave. They
thought he had brought the terrible disease
upon us. They killed him to save the lives of
those yet left, but the whites fell upon us and
killed many more than the disease had taken.
During the summer, two of our men have been
wickedly slain by the whites, but we have not
avenged their death. Our cattle have been stolen ; the penalty is death, if one Indian steals
from another. We have let the white man go
free. In the war, when the pale-faces rained
down upon us, many more of our men than
theirs were killed. You have many times
avenged the death of the missionary."

"Do not get my temper aroused, man!

Would you be shot down like dogs? If not, surrender the men who were engaged in the massacre."

"That I cannot do. One young man might
have killed him, two young men, I do not know,
— it was night. The men did not wish to kill
the missionary ; they begged him to go home."

"Surrender the murderers. Do you see these
men? They are here to obey my orders. If I
tell them to fire into your village, they will kill
you all ; these are but a few — there is another
detachment a mile from here. We are not
responsible for any Indians that the bad white
men around here may kill; we are not here
to talk about bad white men — we have come
to deal with you. It will be death to you all, if
you refuse to surrender these men."

"There are good white men, but they bear no
proportion to the bad," said Sawyer, slowly,
hopelessly ; "the bad must be the strongest, for
they rule." Then fiercely, "You would enslave
those who are not of your own color, although
created by the same Great Spirit. You would
make slaves of us ; you cannot, so you kill us.
You are not like the Indians, who are only ene-
mies in war. You take us by the hand and say
'my friend,' 'my brother' ; only now you took
of our food, yet you would destroy us. You
want to put your foot upon our necks and grind

our faces in the dust.   We have spared the long
knife.   We have suffered much in support of
the whites.   We love our country.   We have
endured much.   Misery encompasses our fami-
lies.   I am the chief, but not the only one in
my nation; there are other chiefs who raise
their crests by my side.   I will call a council
and tell them you wish to murder our men —"

"Not murder your men," interposed the Governor, hastily; "we will take three of your men
back with us and give them a fair trial in the
courts; if guilty, they shall be hung; if nothing
is proved against them, you will see them back
soon.   This must be done to satisfy the citizens, otherwise they and the soldiers will come
down here and wipe your village out of existence."

"The good Father at Washington sent you?"
queried Sawyer.

But the irony fell short of the fat Governor,
and he replied, pompously, "I represent to you
the Father at Washington."

There was great commotion in the village as
the short, pompous Governor wheeled with his
men and left what, an hour before, had been a
quiet, hopeful, expectant community; now, he
had said if the men were not surrendered the
village would be wiped out of existence.   The
Indians were not afraid to fight, but it meant

that men, women and helpless children would
be slain or taken prisoners ; they would have to
leave the homes they had worked hard to make
like the white man's ; they must leave the country that they loved ; all the work of past years
would be for naught ; they must wander in a
strange land. As a people, they were not in-
debted to the United States for either food or
raiment ; thus far they had refused to sign trea-
ties, thus far they had taken care of themselves ;
they had been the friend of the white man —
now they were to experience the white man's
gratitude.

There were sad hearts in the homes that day,
as the men left for the council ; the ploughs left
vacant in the field, the cattle lowing in the corral long before the accustomed time, the women
trying to busy themselves about household cares,
striving to work away the heavy sorrow gnawing
at their hearts, the children sitting idle by the
door-steps, the school-house benches put aside
while stalwart men and some wise women spoke
in council.

That tall man, with the furrowed lines upon
the face, and shoulders slightly bent about the
narrow chest, is Lapwar ; near him sits Medina ;
she has been called the war woman of her tribe,
and the men are always glad to listen to her
wise sayings. Another Indian, whom we have

seen before, is White Swan, the tall son of Sawyer; yet another, Creekie. Among them all,
there is no handsomer face; he has the straight,
aquiline nose, the jet-black eyes, the thin lips,
the slender form of a pure Indian; about his
mouth is an expression that once seen is never
to be forgotten, a sweetness induced by suffering overcome, a firmness denoting strong purpose, a force implying sudden action.

When Sawyer first told them of his interview
with the Governor they would hear of nothing
but war; their hope was to die fighting, rather
than be driven from their village; but when
Sawyer pictured the desolation of their homes,
their farms laid waste, their children slain or
perhaps taken prisoners and subjected to a
worse fate, their wild revenge subsided, hope of
victory vanished, dread despair took its place.
The simple people loved their country, loved
their homes; they listened hopelessly, quietly,
to the cruel proposition made by the Governor.

In the desperate silence that followed, Sawyer
spoke with the dignity of a warrior, with the love
of a father for helpless children, saying : "If you
will go out to war, you shall not go without me.
I have thought of peace measures, it is true, but
only to save my tribe from destruction. A few
of us may be willing to die for our nation — let
these go with the Governor that the rest may

live, may keep their homes, and live in the land
of their forefathers. But if you think me wrong,
if you insist on fighting — go ! and I will go with
you. I will lead you on. I will place myself in
the front. I will fall with the first of you. The
struggle will be great. We must be valiant and
resolute. You can do as you choose, but, for
me, I shall not survive my nation. I will not
live to survive the destruction of so brave a people, who deserve, as you do, a better fate."

Then up sprang Creekie. "It is better a few
of us should die to save the nation, to save our
village from destruction and the pitiless hand of
the white man. Who of you will go to save the
people ? Who of you will die like dogs ? Have
no hearing, no justice; for we have proven the
faith of the white man. Who, for his people, is
willing to be shut out forever from the happy
hunting-grounds ? Who of you will give a life
for the nation ?"

There was no prolonged silence as a few men
slowly arose, but instantly seven men sprang to
their feet ; then others arose, old men with wives
and children, young men with the possibility of
joyous years, each ready to cast aside, forever,
the beckoning future, willing to renounce all
happiness in the future world, knowing that the
Indian who is ignominiously strangled is forever
debarred from the happy hunting-grounds.

A look of pain, and then a look of triumph, crossed Medina's face as she saw Lapwar rise, but suddenly death seemed to have touched her heart, and, with the rest, she tottered from the school-room, for Sawyer had asked that the first seven men who arose might be left alone with him.

When the door had closed upon the people, a silence akin to death reigned within; the horror of the situation crept through their very nerves.

The stronger power had said death for a few of them, or death for all. We are that stronger power. The Indians who fight, we seek to pacify with food and raiment, slight though it be, but Indians such as these we are among, we seek to crush; as Sawyer has said, "We seek to grind their faces in the dust." The foot of Liberty is pressed upon their neck. "You are our wards," we cry; "you shall not have our laws!"

The old fashion among these Indians had been to decide questions of moment while smoking the long-handled pipe; people about to perform some daring deed were selected by fate; the one in whose hand the pipe went out must accomplish the deed; but this custom had passed away soon after their adoption of the white man's dress and mode of living.

To-day, Creekie took upon himself the privilege of passing the fatal slips. It was decided that three of the men must go with the Governor, four would remain in the village. While they were talking, Creekie had prepared and placed in his hat seven slips of common paper, — three bore the death mark, four were blank.

What thoughts must have besieged his brain in these terrible moments! Among the seven were the lover and the father of Suzette. Perchance White Swan would get a slip with death upon it, and Creekie, remaining behind, might yet win the love of Bending Willow; did Lapwar take a fatal slip, who would care more tenderly for his desolate family than Creekie? Even great heroes hear the tempter's voice.

Creekie was coming slowly forward; he had so arranged the slips that he knew where each fatal one lay. First, he passed the hat to White Swan, watching him breathlessly as he saw his hand deliberately seek the fatal slip.

Suddenly, Creekie dropped the hat, the slips were scattered about the floor; hastily he gathered them up, one he tucked in his pocket, one he left face downward at the feet of White Swan, saying, as he passed, "It is fair. That is yours."

White Swan stooped, his eyes fell upon a blank slip.

With trembling heart, Creekie passed on to Lapwar; he had so mixed the slips in picking them up that he knew not one from the other; he knew only that but two death slips remained. Lapwar looked at his slip with face unchanged, and Creekie, not knowing whether Suzette's father had received a fatal slip or not, went on with slow step and sad heart. The silence of the grave was not more deep than that which reigned among these men.

Sawyer gave the signal, and the freed men, who a moment before had stood upon the ragged edge of their own graves, left the room, almost reluctantly. Then the old chief, with bowed head and bursting heart, prayed for the doomed men. He asked God to guard their homes and children; he besought the Great Spirit to give them justice, and he prayed, "Forgive us our debts as we forgive our debtors."

A deep "Amen" came from the hearts of Lapwar and John Lone, but Creekie's lips refused to form the word; his heart could not yet hold that amen.

An hour had passed and Creekie found himself, he knew not why, walking toward the house of Lapwar. Suddenly Suzette sprang before him, her eyes red with weeping, her long hair falling loose about her shoulders, her very lips white.

"Tell me — tell me," she said, "how many —" Her sobs checked her voice. At sight

of her tears Creekie could scarce command his
voice, and, trembling, he answered, "Three."

"And — and —" Her lips made motion, but
they could not form the words.

Creekie knew what she would say ; tenderly
he took her hands between his own, saying,
with gentle voice, "White Swan is safe, Suzette."

Joy rose to her eyes. She did not dream that
Creekie's love for her had been the price of
White Swan's life.

"Tell me," she said, "the names, the names!"

Creekie had never wavered in the council,
had never faltered in his strong purpose ; but
now his lips quivered, and he said, "John Lone
is one to go." He was softly smoothing back
her long hair : he might touch that dark hair
now, he might breathe close to those wide eyes
he loved. He was looking upon Bending Willow for the last time.

"Poor, poor John Lone," she moaned, "his
child is ill, it will kill her."

"Better so, better so," he said, slowly, thinking that heaven was near at hand for the child.

"But another?" she asked, fearfully.

"Ah, Suzette! my poor wounded child, my
poor little Suzette." He held her head back,
looked long into her dark eyes, then said gently,
"Courage! you have the heart of a brave wo-

man.   If your whole nation demanded your
life, could you not give it, Suzette?   Be brave
— be brave —"   But his own eyes filled with
tears and his voice shook.

"You need not tell me," she said, looking
with dazed sight before her; her hands loosened from his and she turned slowly away:
"You need not tell me — it is my father."

"Suzette, Suzette," he cried; he did not
know that his arms were held out to her, he did
not know of the anguish in his own face, and
Suzette only remembered the Creekie of her
childhood,— the kind, sympathizing, warm friend
to whom she had often gone with her girlish
sorrows; he folded her in his arms and she
sobbed her grief upon his breast.

"You must be brave, Suzette," he said; "try
to think of others, little one.   Remember, he
goes to save his people; he goes to save those
he loves."   His voice was growing strong now,
and the girl was trying to be brave and stifle
her sobs.   "It is because he loves you better
than his life, my dear one."   He softly kissed
her dark hair and put her gently from him, saying: "Courage! others are left; think of Medina.   Go, comfort her.   The Good Father keep
you in his care.   The Good Father fill your
home with love and peace."   His hand was

raised in blessing, his face was drawn, his lips tightly closed.

She could not speak, but turned and slowly obeyed his bidding, so slowly that years seemed to have passed over Creekie's face before she was out of sight. Years? Aye, centuries, for in one moment the heart may be cleft in twain. Resolve is the first step, but the hard tearing out of the heart-strings may be the second.

Bending Willow went back to her desolate home; she had not asked the third name; her father's name had been the name of thirty; and Creekie turned, but it was not of his nation that he thought now, this man who had deliberately chosen death. He was thinking of Suzette as a child, Suzette as a woman, and the long years to come when Suzette might be a happy mother. Would it grieve her to think he was one of the three who went to meet—what? He had met his death. Henceforth he must be the warrior—he straightened himself, he threw his head back, but the sunlight blinded him, the notes of the birds jarred upon his ears. He clasped his hands and prayed, prayed only that he might yet live; live to see the joy of Suzette. The birds sang joyously, the sun rose higher in the heavens. Black Hawk stood before him; he came with a message from Sawyer. The Governor and the men were waiting for Creekie. Patrick Lanigan wished to start at once.

Creekie went silently to the house of Sawyer. His erect form renewed the courage of the other men, his sweet smile recalled to them their pride ; their one thought was to die as became warriors.

An hour since, John Lone had entered his poor little shabby home and been met at the door by his young wife ; she had been at home all day with a sick child and neither heard nor knew what was going on — no one had the heart to tell her. "I am glad you have come, John," she said ; "the child has been calling for you. You were gone long," she ventured, gently.

He did not answer the implied rebuke ; he went into the room where the sick child lay.

The poor, wasted form would have called tears to the eyes of a less tender heart than that of the Christian, John Lone. He bent gently and kissed her, and a smile came over the child's wan face as she slowly opened her eyes and rested them on her father ; she was too ill to speak. Her hand stole into his and she closed her eyes, satisfied.

"Don't you think she is better?" asked the wife, anxiously.

But John did not answer, his hungry eyes sought the face of his child.

"You do think she is better?" said Liddie, crowding nearer and placing her hand upon his shoulder.

"The Good Lord will take care of his own," he said, slowly withdrawing his hand from that of the child, who had fallen into a feverish sleep. "Come, Liddie," he said, gently leading his wife away, "come, I have something to say to you." But when he had taken her into the next room his heart failed him, he could not tell her all that had happened in the short time since he had left his home this day; there are limits to all endurance and bravery.

"I am going to leave you for a little time, Liddie," he said. "The Governor of the Territory came to our village this morning. He wants to take a few of us away with him, — away to a large city. We are going down in the boat. Creekie and Lapwar are going."

"You will not leave me and the child, not when the child is ill?" she pleaded, in wide-eyed alarm.

"It is hard to leave you and the child now." His voice almost broke, but he controlled himself with an effort.

"She calls for you when you are gone! What

shall I do? You will not go? You cannot go and leave me and the child—"

"Listen! If a great war were to come upon our people, if by going with the Governor I might help to avert it, would you not say go?"

"No, no. There are others, let them go."

"You will forgive me, Liddie. I have no choice. We drew lots to see who should go."

"But you will return soon?"

He turned his face away.

She put a hand on either of his shoulders and, looking up in his face, repeated her question.

"It may be many days before I return. It may be we part only for a little while, it may be —longer. I have not been as good to you as I might," he said, placing his arms about her. "There are many things I might have done. You know my love for you and our child. You will tell the child I loved her." He paused. "You will teach her to pray—tell her to pray for me. If I should never—" But he thrust his wife aside and hurried from the house. Without one farewell to his child, without one backward glance at his wife, he hastened to the house of Sawyer; there, he begged some of the women to break the sad news to her. "For," he said, mournfully, "the heart of a coward is here," placing his hand upon his breast. "The heart of a warrior is crushed. I cannot tell her." His grief was pitiful. But he cautioned, "You will let her hope. Let her hope I will return, for a little time. It will smooth the edge of her despair. Let her hope for a little, till the child is better. Then tell her all. She will live for the child."

Medina had been truly called the war woman of her tribe. Although at first overcome by the thought that Lapwar was to go, she soon roused herself and with a warrior's pride burst forth : —

"Show the white men of what stuff the Indian is made. They may kill your body, but they cannot crush your spirit. They will see how warriors can die. Your names will be handed down to your children. You are the heroes of your nation. Oh ! that I were a man, to go with you." And she cried to the men, as with noble mien and heads unbent they passed out of the village : "They are cowards who would make you die ; show them what bravery is. Die like Indians, like warriors."

Aye, but the desolate village when the sun withdrew his rays that night ; the desolation, the heart-break, the bitter wailing, the despair !

The Governor pushed on through the night in his boats till darkness fell like a hideous pall. The Indians were put on shore while the white men slept in the boats. One guard was placed over these Indians. Think you they could not escape? Nothing easier than to knock the guard senseless and fly through the woods; but they had given their word.

Do not blame the men who had accompanied the Governor; they were soldiers, they merely obeyed their superiors, they were under oath, they did as they were bid.

A sickening, howling crowd met these Indians as they landed at Devil City, and through this miserable, jeering, taunting crowd they passed with heads erect to the jail.

They were tried in a language they did not understand, they were found guilty by a court which allowed them no chance for defence.

The Indians listened with immovable faces when their sentence was pronounced.

There was no murmur of despair, no sigh of regret, as with the majesty of heroes they walked slowly to the gallows.

They were hung, amid the jeers and hurrahs of civilized American children, women and men in this enlightened nineteenth century. Did Liberty veil her eyes?

Look back at the village of despairing people! Look to this crowd of our boasted civilization! Look to these three men of Wallowa, mangled at the foot of the gallows and tell me, shall we give the Indian our law? Which are the savages, they who vent their law upon these men of Wallowa, or they who died without the protection of the law? Let Creekie, John Lone, and Lapwar speak to you from their graves.

SAMUEL, AN ARAPAHOE.

I HAVE heard that there are a good many white people who know nothing of the wrongs which have been done to our people and would like to hear a little of them ; I believe the Great Spirit is going to pity the Indian.

I have been asked to tell my story in my own way. It is a poor way, but for the sake of White Doe I will tell it.

My people call me Branching Pine, because I am tall and straight, with heavy, short hair that flies out in stiff tufts and nods in the blowing breeze like the top branches of the swaying pine; but in the prison-book I am Samuel, an Arapahoe.

White Doe is slender and timid. No one knows why she gave herself to a big fellow like me. White Doe is brave ; she will bite her lips and keep back the tears though her heart breaks. She has little, brown hands that lose themselves in my black, bushy hair. Her large, soft eyes would make a man good and brave, just for the look of love and trust in them. I did well until she was dying, — dying. Then my heart leapt to my throat, my blood rushed through my body, till my soul was on fire. I would have killed any one that stood in the way of White Doe's life.

But I am all a-tremble. I cannot tell my story unless I begin at the beginning.

It warms my heart to think of my home again, with the clean, dirt floor and the window high in the wall for the sun to shine through, and the neat roof of close-packed earth with the grass growing up on the edge. In the field, White Doe and I work side by side until she leaves me to go in and get the evening meal ; I hear her voice through the open door as she sings the songs they taught at the school ; then the red sun sets, and that is the last happy day that we know.

To go back and tell you of the misery of my people would make your heart ache, if you are a true man or a true woman.

Many promises were made us by too many people ; we believed them, but the Indian has learned to know the white man better. We lived in a broad country with much game, but the white man set his foot upon our country and the game fled. Because we let the white man go through our country and own land, the Great

Father called a council, and for the right of way through our country, and because the white man scattered our game, he promised us each a dollar a year for fifty years, and we promised to be at peace. But the Great Father at Washington thought again, and took back his promise. He gave us each a dollar for fifteen years, and the Indian kept his peace with the white man, though he came and took rich mines on our land that we were not taught to work. The great travel sent the buffalo away. We had nothing with which to kill the small game. They would not let us go to hunt the buffalo away off where the white man did not tread, and we were starving. The Great Father promised to teach us to be farmers, but I think he must have forgotten.

The women were pinched with want and the children crying with hunger. We begged for a farmer or a blacksmith, but it was years before the Father at Washington remembered us. Other Indians stole horses and cattle, they stole food, and killed the white man, and the Great Father thought them brave. We were starving while we kept our faith with the white men.

What I say here is true. You may kill me, but do not say what I tell here is a lie ; and this is how it happened. A number of young men were weary of starving, just to be at peace with the white man who had forgotten his promise,

so they went to make war on a hostile tribe that
was always our enemy. They did not go to
make war on the white man.

When they were in camp the mail wagon
passed and two young men went out to beg to-
bacco, but the mail carrier fired on them so the
Indians fired back, and that is the way it was.
The carrier fired on the young men who had
gone out in a friendly spirit. The chief ran out
and stopped the firing. He brought the two
men into camp and flogged them. He said the
white man would say they had broken the peace,
even although they were not the first to fire.

The mail man went to the fort and told a
strange thing, for the soldiers came down and
fired on us and killed many. The chief could
no longer control the war spirit of Indians
who saw their friends killed by soldiers, after
they had thrown down their bows and arrows
and said there should be peace, so a war followed.

After this our chiefs went into a great council
and said they would kill any young man who
tried to go on the war-path. Some of the young
men were killed.

A white chief came and demanded our men
who had taken part in the war. Peace had come
and we would not give them up; then the white
chief burned our village and destroyed our food.
Suffering and sorrow visited us through the long

winter. The white chief did not remember that we had kept our faith when the whites had forgotten theirs. He only remembered that now he was the stronger power. The Great Spirit had forgotten us. We went to hunt buffalo, but could hardly find any. We had to kill a good many of our ponies to eat, to save ourselves from starving. The children got sick and died. A great many of our finest young men died, as well as many women. Then the governor chief sent out to call all friendly Indians into the fort, because there was to be a great war, and he told us we would be safe. He said he would protect us because we had kept our promises. They gave us food. Then they moved us some miles from the fort so that we would be better protected.

My mother could have told what happened. When daylight came, the troops fell upon us and murdered our men, women, and children. My mother fled with me over the prairie. When my father ran to the troops and begged them not to fire, they shot him dead. The head chief carried a white flag, and when he saw what had come upon us, that there was no mistake, it was a planned attack, he folded his arms and waited till he was shot down. Young men and old women, old men and little children, were murdered; their fingers were cut off, their legs and

arms broken, their ears cut off. It makes my
heart sick to remember my mother's words and
to hear what she saw before she carried me, a
little child, in her arms and fled.

This was the faith of the white man.

The Indian was a fool-man who kept peace
with them. They held out their hand in peace,
and when we took it, they stabbed us in the
back.

After this it was hard to believe white men
any more. We were afraid we would be be-
trayed again. Now we are afraid no longer.
We come and take the white man by the hand
once more, — it is better to be at peace.

They gave my mother 160 acres of land, and
to me, because they murdered my father, they
gave the same. Did they think it would bring
my father back from the spirit world? Did they
think the land could take the place of a father
and husband? We had plenty of land before
the white men came. They took our land,
murdered my father, and then gave us back a
little piece of land to make us happy. Did they
think because we had the land that we were satisfied that he was murdered? Did they think
it would dry my mother's tears, or ease the pain
at her heart? Some people think because we
are of a different complexion, we are not men
and women.

We were no longer allowed to hunt and we had no implements to work the ground. We used axes, sticks of wood, and worked with our hands in the earth to prepare our ground for planting. We had a few cattle; but the white man ran them off and we were not allowed to go after them.

When my mother died, White Doe and I came to live in the house I had built. We had suffered many years from giving up our own way of living and trying to live as the white man, with nothing to do it with, and no one to show us how. The white man did not learn in a day, neither can the Indian.

We did not know how to work the field at first, and the man who came to show us did not know either. To-day he would tell us one way, and to-morrow he would tell us another, and we were worse off than before. He was old and feeble and the work was not good for him. Soon the Great Father at Washington sent him off. The Great Father does not allow his children to remain in one place long. Just when we understand, he sends them away.

The Great Father wants us to stay in one place forever, but he changes his own children all the day. Where did the Great Father get his authority to say to us, "Stay in one place;" and to the white man, "Go where you please,

only stay on a reservation until you begin to do
your work, then go on"? I have asked many
men, but they cannot tell me.

The next man who came to show us could
not understand our language. We had not been
taught the English language in the school, so
we could not understand him. There was no
interpreter and it took a long time for us to
learn, and a great patience before he could
teach us.

After a few years we succeeded in farming,
but there was no one to buy our produce, so we
could get no money. We had food enough to
eat, but no money to buy any clothes.

There were few farm implements. We had
to wait our turn to use them, for we had no
money to buy others. We lost part of our crop
because we could not get it in in time.

White Doe and I had a neat little plat. We
had enough to eat and enough to carry food to
our sick neighbor, and we thought the white
man's way a good way.

But the last year we worked our field and
nothing would come. The sun shone hot and
died in a red ball at night, no rain came to
quench the earth, everything withered and died.
It was hard to keep a brave heart.

There was much sickness in our village.
Many people died because there was no medi-

cine for them. We were always hungry. We
never had enough. When they that were sick
felt they could eat something, we had nothing
to give them.

A white chief came from Washington. He
said our land had not been marked out right and
it did not belong to us. Our homes were to be
taken from us. Why did not the white man
mark it right at first? Why did he wait until we
had built a home and worked the land? Was it
not enough that we were starving? Was it not
enough that we were dying? Surely the Great
Spirit had hidden his face from us. We had no
longer heart to go into the field and work.
Many of our relatives and friends died. We
felt that we would like to be asleep with the
rest. But I, for the sake of White Doe, worked
in the field. I did not want her to realize that,
after all her work and plans, she had no home
on the face of the earth ; and she, for my sake,
came and worked by my side to make me forget
our wrong, to make me forget our sorrow. She
would laugh and sing as though she were
happy, but often I would see tears upon her
cheeks as she laughed. My heart ached that I
was powerless to help her. Why could we not
be treated as other men? Why could we not
have a home? Why could they not give us an
even chance to live as other men? We would

be content if we had an even chance with the
white man. It makes my heart sick to remember all the promises of the white man; to remember our own country where we had plenty
to eat, where we had a home, and now to see my
people cooped up like chickens, their food taken
from them, their houses delivered to others, no
even chance in the law. If this is the kind of
guardian that brings this upon us, we want no
guardian. We want to be free men to have an
even chance in the law. We know we must
change. We are willing to adopt the white
man's way, but the Great .Father is always
changing. He puts us here; he puts us there.
This man is put over us and when we know this
man's way the Great Father takes him off and
puts another man over us and we learn a different
way. How would a child do, if it had thirty
mothers a month, each day a different mother?
Would the child grow and prosper? No more
can the Indian. I wish the Great Father at
Washington would remember and think of this.

The Great Father must think we are made
different from other men.

The night when the sun went down so red,
the night I remember so well, we had been
making believe that this was our own home
once more, that this land we had worked was
ours; that we had enough to eat and to give our

neighbor. White Doe had laughed as she ran into the house and we had much merriment over our last bit of meal and salt. Her merriment lightened my heart. There were bright spots in her cheeks and a brightness in her eyes that did my heart good, for she had looked pale of late.

When I slept that night I dreamed that we were travelling the white man's road content.

But in the morning she muttered strange things. I thought she was asleep, but her eyes were open wide. The red spots burned in her cheeks. I trembled under the weight of this mighty sorrow. White Doe was ill of the fever. Her lips were parched with thirst, her hands were hot and dry. She begged for food. I hid my face in my hands, for I had none to give her. A fierce pain clutched at my heart when I heard this cry of hunger that I could not help. My nails sank into the palms of my hands until the flesh bled. All about us the white man had plenty, but my dear one lay ill of a fever and I had nothing to give her. I bathed her brow and hands in cold water. I smoothed back her hair and spoke in a soft voice. Soon her moaning ceased, her eyes closed in sleep.

Then I went for old Matilda. She came and watched by the side of White Doe and I went forth with sad heart.

Blackfoot was the pony that my dear one loved. It had some of the gentle ways of White Doe and raised its glad eyes in mute welcome as I came and led it out into the yard. We had always divided our food with Blackfoot, but to-day there was nothing for her. The dry stalks of grass had long since ceased to give her any nourishment. When she stuck her moist nose in my empty hand I could only pat her head and tell her she must carry me swift. She whinnied and crooked her neck to look for White Doe. I think the dumb beast knew there was something wrong, for my dear one had always come out to her the first thing in the morning. I sprang upon her sleek back and pressed my feet against her side and away she sped with me over the prairie. In our home lay my dear one starving and parched with fever. I would have killed myself that she might live, yet I could not help her. I groaned aloud when I thought of our misery.

Before the sun sank in the west I was near my home again. Blackfoot had carried me swift and sure to the door of the white medicine man. He gave me fair words, but that would not bring White Doe back to health. He could not come to see her, he had no wagon, no horse. I told him to mount Blackfoot, but he said the Indian's pony was full of tricks. I told him

to get on Blackfoot, and I would lead her
all the way. He said it would take too much
time. He had to tend his sick at home. I said
I would work for him night and day for nothing, after White Doe was.well, if he would only
come. I said I would give him Blackfoot, he
could sell her and take the money, if he would
but come. He said if he had a horse and team
of his own he would come. The Great Father
furnished him none. He could not come. He
said to give her nourishing drinks. He might
have told me to shoot the stars, or make the
moon square.

Why does the Great Father at Washington
send us a physician and give him no way of
coming to us when we are sick? I think the
Great Father forgets many things.

His words were fair, but White Doe lay ill
and he would not come to help us. There was
no food and he said she must have nourishing
drinks. No one would help us. White Doe
must have something to nourish her and there
was nothing.

Out on the prairie there, no one would
notice the report of a rifle. There was a
stake near, made ugly and black by the prairie fire. Blackfoot looked at me with wide
eyes when I tied her bridle to it. She had
never been tied up before. She had never

strayed beyond her lariat rope. She was breathing hard and the steam rose from her strained
flanks.

Then I went up and spoke gently to her.
We had brought her up from a colt. White
Doe and I loved her next to each other. When
I went off a few paces, she tugged at her rope
to be free and whinnied to me. I went back
and spoke gently to her. I twined my fingers
in her mane and leant my cheek against her
face. I patted her shiny neck. Then again I
stood a few paces off ; her mild eyes looked at
me in wonder as I raised my rifle to my shoulder. Never shall I forget her look of human
reproach. I shut my eyes and pulled the trigger — the bullet went crunching — crunching —

She made one mad leap, then fell to the
ground. She moaned like a human child and
moved her head near me where I had dropped
on my knees before her. My hot tears fell
upon her face. I had killed my dearest friend,
next to White Doe. With broken voice I tried
to tell the dumb creature why I had done this.
I could not bear the look in her mild eyes.

I would have died that White Doe might live,
yet I must live to take care of my dear one.
Blackfoot could die and nourish my poor, sick
one. It would have been easier to run a knife
into my breast than to stand and kill our faith-

ful Blackfoot, White Doe's friend and playmate;
now she lay stiff and motionless before me.
Never more would she bear my dear one over
the rolling prairie ; never more would her moist
nose seek my hand for a caress; never more
would she prick her ears and whinny at our
approach ; never more would she hear the voice
of White Doe.   Forever more should I see the
look in her hazel eyes as I raised my gun to kill
her.

I dragged myself home and told old Matilda
what I had done.   Some one else must do the
rest.   I could do no more ; so Matilda went and
told Beverlie.   He was the friend of White Doe
and me.   He did the rest.

Then I sat by the side of White Doe.   She
was asleep and breathing heavily.   When Matilda asked me where was the medicine man,
and where was the medicine, I could not answer
her.   I turned my face away.

Near me was some meal and water; some one
had brought it for White Doe to drink.   I had
had no food that day, but while I sat there a
kind neighbor brought me a potato, which I
eagerly ate.   I must keep up my strength for
the sake of White Doe.

In the morning, White Doe knew me.   I
gave her some hot soup to drink.   Her eyes
brightened at sight of it, and while she sipped

it she said, "Where did this come from?" And
I answered, "Beverlie brought it," for had he
not finished my work?

Then she said, "Poor Blackfoot! is there
nothing for her? What have you given her?"

I steadied my voice and answered, "Blackfoot
has plenty," for I knew she was now beyond
suffering and want. But old Matilda came,
and stood in the open door, and she said, "Be
not foolish; Blackfoot is killed to nourish you,
and that is —" But White Doe screamed.
The bowl dropped from her fingers and she fell
back as one dead.

Then I cried, "You are the fool!" to Matilda,
and rushed to the side of White Doe. She lay
still and pale a long time. When she opened
her eyes, she was raving — raving. She would
scream out, "Blackfoot, Blackfoot, I have killed
you," and then sink shivering under the bed-
clothes. "Come, Blackfoot, dear Blackfoot,"
and she would stroke her hand as though she
touched Blackfoot's shiny neck; then she would
start back, her eyes full of terror, screaming,
"Take your eyes away! Yes; it was I, I that
killed you," and I would sit there trying to
soothe her till my heart was nearly dead within
me. The fever had seized her stronger than
before and now there was no nourishment for
her.

Matilda wept and was sorry, but she could not undo her foolishness.

The work that Beverlie had done, I gave to him and his family, for now White Doe knew; and I would never touch it anyway.

You, who have food and plenty, do not know what it is to be hungry. You do not know what it is to see your sick cry out for food you cannot give. You do not know the pain of it. I would have been a fool-man to sit with my head in my hands while my dear one lay sick for want of food. For what I had given Beverlie, he sent me some meal, but a handful of meal in water would not nourish White Doe.

My people were all starving. Others had suffered as we were suffering now, but it is different when the misery creeps under your own roof. It is different when the dearest one on earth lies ill; it is different when she raises her eyes to yours in want, and the thing that she needs lies all about you, yet she must die for lack of it. If you were a weakling like the sick one — very well — but when you are a strong man you cannot sit still. The Great Spirit knows whether I did right or not. It would have been easier to kill White Doe than to see her slowly die while I stood helpless. I strode from the house. My mind was fixed. I could bear it no longer.

My friend Beverlie went with me. Over the
prairie and away to the mountains we went.
We had offered to work for the white man if he
would give us meat, but he would not. We had
nothing to give but the work of our hands.
This was our country. If the white man had
treated us fair we would not have been starving.
If we had been allowed to go in pursuit of our
cattle that the white man ran off from our herd,
we would have had some cattle now.

What we did, we did in the broad light of
day. We did not, like the white man, wait for
the covering of night. We were desperate,
starving men, and my loved one was dying for
what the white man might have given in mercy.
Blackfoot would have carried me swift. I killed
her that I might not take from the white man as
he had taken from us.

It is true that Beverlie and I killed the ox.
We carried as much of it away as we could. I
believe the Great Spirit is looking down on all
of us, and for that reason I am telling the truth.

White Doe had nourishment that night, and
I did not shrink from telling her what we had
done. Is there a man or woman of you who
would not have done the same? We were no
cowards.

The next day came men to carry Beverlie and
me to prison.

There lay the sick dear one. But the Christian white men did not care for that. She moaned and cried when they dragged me away. But the Christian white men did not care for that.

News was brought to White Doe that every one at the agency sympathized with us. The poor dear one thought they would free us, and give us food. But, when she found we were to go to the prison, she cried out and said she would no longer have the religion of the white man, and I cannot but think she was right.

The white man has had many years of your religion, yet he lies to us, he cheats us, he kills us. You tell me that your religion is to do to your brother as you would he did to you, yet the white man says, " Kill all the Indians." Are we not brothers with one Father above us ?

They locked us in prison. My heart did not break, for I thought I should be near my dear one. I could hear how she was. I could send her word. Some one would sometimes come and tell me how she was and what she said, but they sent us off from the Territory. They sent us over a waste of country to a strange land and put us behind iron bars.

I did not feel the shackles that I wore. I did not feel the heavy irons sinking about my legs. The iron was in my heart. White Doe lay

dying. They bound Beverlie and me together
with heavy chains, and burdened our feet with
irons.

White Doe sleeps, never to awake.

White man, do not hold out your hand to me
and speak of friendship.   The body of White
Doe lies between us.   Do you think your hand
could reach me over *that*?

My heart is heavy.   I hope that I, too, shall
soon sleep in peace.

You took my food from me, and when I had
learned to toil, you stole the home I had built
with my hands and the ground I had worked
hard to make like the white man's garden.
You put me in iron chains and brought me to
prison.   I do not say I am innocent.   I did take
an ox that Beverlie and I found in the mountain; and the man who stole my cattle and
branded them with his mark claimed the ox as
his; but had your law been right, that man
should have been in prison seven times, for
those are the number of cattle he took from
me; but he is a white man, and I an Indian.
You are a rich nation.   You have conquered
a brave people.   We do not want to fight.
The white man has taken away everything.   I
hope some day the white man will do justice
to the Indian.   I want to say that I only ask
for justice.

They tell me that your nation is governed by the will of the people. After much thought, I make out that, because the white man has learned your will, he can steal from the Indian, he can ruin his home, he may kill him ; but the law that you use will not punish the white man. I do not see that we have been benefited in the least by all your laws. Is this your will? I want to say again that I only ask for justice. Give the Indians an even chance with the white men. Treat them as men and women. I can say no more. I speak to-day ; perhaps to-morrow I die.

www.ingramcontent.com/pod-product-compliance
Lightning Source LLC
Chambersburg PA
CBHW021124020726
47500CB00003B/917